# THE SON
# OF TARZAN

This is the fourth
story in the Tarzan series

D1438066

*By the same author*
*All in the Dragon series*

TARZAN OF THE APES
THE RETURN OF TARZAN
THE BEASTS OF TARZAN

Published by arrangement with Western Publishing
Company, Inc., Racine, Wisconsin, U.S.A.

*The Son of Tarzan*
was first published in the U.K.
in 1919 by Methuen & Co., Ltd. and
has been reprinted twenty-five times.
This edition, adapted for a younger
readership, was published in 1967 by
Atlantic Book Publishing Co. Ltd.,
11 New Fetter Lane, London E.C.4.
It was printed in the U.K. by
C. Nicholls & Company Ltd.
The Philips Park Press, Manchester 11.

# THE SON
# OF TARZAN

## Edgar Rice Burroughs

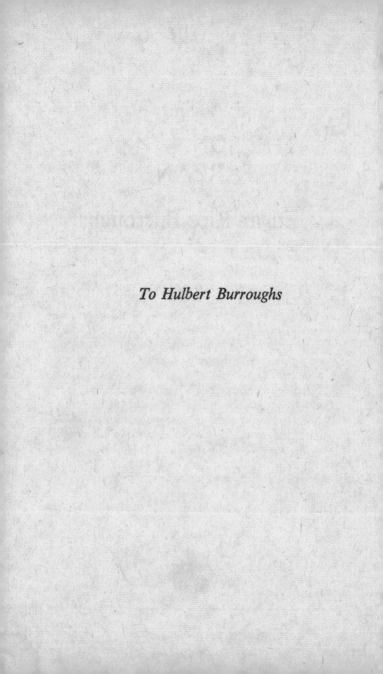

*To Hulbert Burroughs*

# The Man from the Jungle

Out from the jungle came a man, a scarecrow of a creature. He was naked save for a loincloth, and a white beard straggled down his thin chest. He was so gaunt, so skinny, it was painful to see. He stood there, tears rolling down his wasted cheeks.

The men in the longboat rested on their oars, astonished. They had just pulled out from the *Marjorie W.*, an American ship cruising off the coast of Africa on a scientific survey.

"A white man," exclaimed one of the seamen, and at that the scarecrow began to speak, his voice jabbering in a strange tongue.

"A Russian," said the mate, but he knew little of the language. "Savvy English?" he asked.

The scarecrow did. He spoke haltingly, pleading to be taken off the accursed shore of Africa. They landed and crowded round him, giving him food and drink. He seemed ravenous. After a while he told his story.

Years and years before – was it ten or fifteen years? – he had been captured by a native tribe and enslaved. He had been treated frightfully, starved and tormented so that it was a wonder he remained alive. He said his name was Michael Sabrov, but he hesitated so long over the name that the mate was not sure it was his real name or something his tormented brain had thought up.

"Okay," said the mate at length. "We'll take you to the ship."

They took him aboard the *Marjorie W.*, and everyone pitied him. He was clothed and shaved, fed and treated by the ship's doctor. They took him with them because that was all they could do, and one day in the course of their survey they came to a tropical island off the coast of Africa where they landed. Sabrov was taken ashore, to go in camp with the scientists.

One day there was a commotion – a panther had been seen in the long grass. Someone got a gun and shot it, and everyone went across to look at the beautiful beast.

Sabrov alone was uninterested. He had lain himself under a tree and was in a half-doze. Something touched his shoulder. His head came round. Squatting by his side was a huge and hairy ape. Sabrov sat up, terrified but incapable of movement. The ape peered closely into his face, then jabbered something but did not attempt to harm the Russian.

Slowly Sabrov rose to his feet and then began to edge away. The giant ape walked alongside him, still talking in his ape language, and his voice sounded curiously mournful and disappointed.

When the seamen turned and saw the odd pair coming towards them, they scattered at first, and then came closer when they saw the ape meant no harm.

And then an astonishing thing happened. The ape went up to one of the boldest seamen, placed his hands on his shoulders and peered intently into the man's face. Almost the ape seemed to shake his head, and then pass on to the next seaman. Each in turn he scrutinised, and each time he seemed disappointed.

The men were delighted. "Reckon this beast's been tamed by some man at some time or other," said one of the seamen sagely.

But there was a fool in the party, a man not content with friendliness on the part of a dumb animal. He had a long slim knife, and with a grin on his face he came up behind the ape and pricked him in the rear.

The ape was not tame. Like a flash it whirled on the grinning idiot, tore the knife from his grasp and threw it away, then buried its savage fangs in the man's shoulder. Instantly there was uproar, the other seamen trying to rescue their screaming comrade. Roaring with anger the ape lashed out, mighty arms downing men like skittles.

Now the captain and the mate came running up, drawing their revolvers, but suddenly between them and the ape ran the wild man they had rescued. He was screaming, "Stop, stop! The ape is mine!" and his presence was so startling no one fired.

By this time the seamen had rescued their mate so that the ape stood alone in their midst, growling ferociously. The wild man, as if unconscious of fear, went and stood by the side of the ape, calling, "He is mine and he is friendly. He would not have hurt anyone if that man had not pricked him with a knife."

Indeed the ape seemed remarkably docile now, and certainly made no attempt to harm the man at his side. Instead he walked forward, interested in the newcomers. He went close to the mate and peered in his face, and again it seemed as if he shook his head, disappointed. Then he did the same to the captain. And when he had done that he came back to Sabrov and just stood quietly by his side, as if no longer interested in the other men around him.

When they returned to the ship, the ape followed them. He got into the boat and seemed almost on the point of using an oar, but they took it away from him. Aboard ship they found him some old blankets and made him a bed in the tiny cabin given to Sabrov.

"Now, that," said the captain that evening, "is the darndest, queerest thing I've ever seen. Sabrov says the ape's his, eh?"

The mate frowned. "He says so," he admitted, "but I've got a feeling he's never met the ape before." In which he was nearly right.

The captain stopped filling his pipe. "What makes you think that?"

"He didn't call the ape by a name. Now, if the ape had been his pet, the most natural thing for him would be to call him by name, wouldn't it?"

But that night Sabrov was calling the ape by name.

7

Ajax, he called him, though it was days before the ape answered to the name, as if it was something new to him.

A month later the *Marjorie W.* sailed for England, there to drop their British scientists. Sabrov said he wanted to go ashore at London, and the way he said it made the captain think. For Sabrov's eyes glinted insanely as he spoke, as if filled with hatred at the thought of what lay before him in London.

"Queer chap," thought the captain, not for the first time. "Cracked, of course." Who wouldn't be after all those years of torment in the jungle? Aloud he said, "You taking Ajax with you?"

Sabrov said, defiantly, "Ajax is mine."

"Okay, you can have him," said the captain quickly. "But what are you going to do with him?"

And this was something Sabrov had thought of through the many weeks at sea. "I shall put him in a circus. I have no money – he will earn a living for me. And ..."

Sabrov's voice trailed away. "And what?" asked the captain curiously. Sabrov was a long time in replying.

Then suddenly –"And together we will find a man, a man I hate more than anyone else in the world. And when I meet him he will die, and I will make him die slowly, in torment, just as I have been in torment all these years. For that man put me into the hands of those black fiends!"

"Cracked," said the captain again to himself. "Mad as they come."

Undoubtedly he was mad, this Michael Sabrov, and he had always been reckless and violent even before his African experience. It was going to be hard on the man whom he hated more than anyone else on earth, if ever their paths crossed.

That man was Tarzan of the Apes, Tarzan the Mighty.

For Sabrov was not Sabrov. That was a name invented on the spur of the moment. His real name was Alexis

Paulvitch and Tarzan was the one man who had thwarted his criminal designs many years ago.

There was mutiny in the air, and Lord Greystoke faced it with a twinkle in his eye. Before him stood his son, Jack, sturdy and resolute and none the worse for being kidnapped and taken to Africa when a baby.*

In the background Lady Greystoke listened, a smile of pride on her face as she looked at her son. Hovering nervously behind Greystoke was Mr. Moore, a young man rapidly becoming convinced that being private tutor to the son of Lord Greystoke was not the easiest way of earning money.

Jack said, "Everyone's talking about him, father. Willie Grimsby says it's the most wonderful ape anyone's ever seen. It rides a bike, counts up to ten and does amazing tricks."

Lord Greystoke said, softly, "I know how you feel, Jack, but there are reasons why I do not want you to visit a circus."

He and his wife had discussed the matter many times in recent years. Lady Greystoke in particular was uneasy about the situation. "If he knew you were Tarzan of the Apes, it would make him want to go to Africa and try to live as you did," she said, and there she was wise in her knowledge of children. They loved their only son, and the thought of him living, as his father had had to live, with the beasts of the jungle, in constant peril, made them determined to keep him out of Africa at all costs.

"I have a feeling," Tarzan once said to his wife, with a smile, "there is a lot of Tarzan in my son. Call it instinct if you like, but there it is – this feeling that if he knew of my past he would feel the call of Africa."

"We can't have that," said Lady Greystoke quickly,

* See The Beasts of Tarzan

9

so that Jack grew up without realising his father was the legendary Tarzan of the Apes, about which so much had been written not many years before. Tarzan often sighed for the glorious days when he was a jungle man, but now that his life was committed to England and his family – a country estate and a seat in the House of Lords – he stifled those desires, and to please his beloved wife kept them from his son.

Part of their fear lay in Jack's uncanny ability to handle animals, something he had inherited from his brilliant father. Tarzan had watched him and marvelled at the power of Jack's voice to make friends of surly dogs and restive horses. "There's something of me in that boy," Tarzan often thought, and he and his wife long before decided to keep their son away from zoos and circuses – anywhere where African animals were to be seen. African animals – could they exert an influence on the jungle man's son? Neither Lord Greystoke nor his wife could be sure.

Now the problem had risen again. Yet another circus was in the vicinity, this time with a wonderful ape called Ajax. They hated to disappoint the boy, but – "I'm sorry," Lord Greystoke said again. "No circus for you, my son."

And then came the mutiny. Jack's chin tilted. "I am going, father."

"I forbid you," said Tarzan quietly.

"I intend to go."

"You will be punished."

"I will take my punishment," said Jack quite calmly, and went off to his bedroom, leaving his parents proud yet a little uneasy.

When he had gone, Tarzan turned to the dithering young Mr. Moore. "Keep an eye on him," he said.

"An eye?" said Mr. Moore bleakly, very conscious of young Jack's powerful muscles.

"Keep him confined to his room – he must not go to the circus," Tarzan ordered.

10

Mr. Moore blinked behind his glasses and went up-stairs. For a moment he hesitated outside young Jack's room, then carefully opened the door and peeped inside. His eyebrows shot up almost into his hair. Jack was getting away to the circus without any loss of time!

Young Jack was seated astride the window sill, about to climb down a drain-pipe. When he saw his tutor he said, firmly, "Keep away from me and shut your mouth."

But Mr. Moore was more afraid of Tarzan than the son of Tarzan. Yelping like a startled pup he rushed across the room, laid hands on Jack and tried to drag him across the sill. "Your father says you must not go to the circus. Come back!"

Jack sighed. "All right," he said, and clambered back into the room. "If this is the way you want it. . . ."

Mr. Moore was not a big man, but then he was not particularly small. He suddenly found himself lifted by young Jack – lifted so easily that it was marvellous so much strength could be packed into such a youthful frame.

Mr. Moore struggled and cried out. "Shut up," advised Jack, but Mr. Moore had little sense even though he was a tutor. He kept on bleating, "Put me down."

So Jack obliged. He put him down – down on to the bed, face down in a pillow which effectually ended Mr. Moore's agitated cries. A sheet was suddenly pulled under Mr. Moore's face and tied behind his head. He was gagged. A firm hand held him down while another wrapped a sheet round his legs. Then Mr. Moore's hands were tied behind his back.

"I shall return," young Jack promised cheerfully, and the squirming tutor heard sounds from the window as the boy clambered out on his way to a blissful evening at his first circus.

Mr. Moore was very upset. There was the indignity of it – he, a man, had been handled like a child by virtually a schoolboy. True, a remarkable schoolboy, packing more muscle than most adult men even at his tender age.

There was also fear, for Mr. Moore was a fearful young man, afraid of almost everything. Now, squirming on the bed, he was afraid of what Lord Greystoke would say when he found him in this ignominious position. Behind the gag his face flushed red with mortification, and he vowed that when he got free he would not remain another night under the same roof as his wretched pupil.

Mr. Moore squirmed with mingled fear and wrath, squirmed so much that to his alarm he found himself falling off the bed. There was a bump sufficient to shake the house, and it gave him an idea. Raising his bound feet he brought them down with a crash on the floor, an exercise which he repeated at ten second intervals thereafter.

Down below Lord Greystoke looked up from his book and said, "Now, what is young Jack up to?" His wife shook her head wonderingly. So Lord Greystoke rang the bell, and when a footman appeared ordered him to go to Master Jack's room and find out what all the rumpus was about.

Five minutes later a scared footman came back leading a very flustered tutor.

"He's gone!" cried the tutor, getting it in quickly.

"My son?" exclaimed Tarzan, startled. "Gone where?"

"To the circus – to see that wretched Ajax. And I," said Mr. Moore, drawing himself to full height, "am going, too. I tender my resignation, sir. You do not need a tutor for your son, you need an animal trainer."

Tarzan manfully held back his smile, and the tutor swept out. Lord Greystoke looked at his wife. "I think I too will visit the circus," he said, and his instinct told him this was the beginning of big and dramatic events.

## Ajax the Giant Ape

Jack was in a seventh heaven of delight. The circus was dazzlingly wonderful – the lights, the brassy music, the colour and movement were all new to him and a great thrill.

But it was when the animal acts came on that he really sat up in his seat. Just before the interval cages were erected and lions came slinking into the ring. Jack found himself curiously stirred at sight of them, as if deep in his subconscious mind there was an appeal that was linked to his instincts. The lions fascinated him, almost magnetically drawing him out of his seat towards them.

Then the great elephants came on with their act, and again his instincts moved out to them. Curiously it was only the African animals that stirred him – he liked the performing seals and the dancing bear, but they did not rouse in him the same emotions as the African beasts.

Then, right at the end of the show, came the act that everyone was waiting to see – the great Ajax, the almost human ape. When Ajax shambled into the ring, it seemed as if something hit young Jack. He sat bolt upright, his eyes staring at the great, shaggy creature as if willing it to come to him.

The act began. Ajax was truly remarkable. He could count. He could identify objects laid before him – "Find the watch, Ajax" or "Show me the cigarette lighter". He never failed instantly to pick up the article named. Obviously he was of a high order of intelligence among apes and the applause thundered out at each new act of cleverness.

Then came a part of the act where the huge Ajax had to go into the audience. In the ring the trainer would call, "Show me a lady with a blue dress, Ajax," and Ajax would shamble up the aisle until he saw a blue-clad lady and would then point at her. Or – "Point to a man with a brown suit" or "A man smoking a pipe." Ajax never missed, always pointing at the right person.

Jack watched the great ape come closer to his seat, right on the edge of the aisle. He felt that he could hardly breathe, he was so thrilled by the closeness of Ajax.

Then Ajax came right up to him. "Show me a lady wearing a white coat," called the trainer, back in the ring.

But Ajax had stopped playing games. Ajax had halted in front of Jack. For a moment he stood there, peering at the boy, and then all at once he became so excited that people in the seats around stood up in alarm. Not so, Jack – he sat there completely unafraid of the great beast that towered over him, his face alight, his eyes shining.

Ajax laid mighty hairy paws on Jack's shoulders and stared intently into his face. He was talking rapidly, excitedly, and yet to Jack it seemed he was puzzled, unsure about something.

The trainer began to shout to Ajax to come back to the ring. Ajax did not seem to hear him. He was talking to Jack, caressing him. And Jack sat enthralled, oblivious of the commotion around him, as people tried to get away from him and the ape.

A seat came empty next to Jack. Ajax promptly sat down in it, his arm around Jack's shoulders, his face peering closely into the boy's. The trainer was cracking his whip and ordering the ape to return to the ring. The ape ignored him. Some of the audience in delight began to cheer.

The show was being held up. The circus manager, a fat man with a perpetually angry face, came into the ring and began a furious argument with the trainer, pointing to the clock as he did so.

The trainer leapt out of the ring and came up to Ajax.

14

He shouted to the ape to get back in the ring. Ajax went on sitting there, arm around Jack's shoulders, talking softly now in ape language – talking like someone who has searched the world and suddenly found what he has been searching for, someone loved above all others ... and yet puzzled, not sure, something was not quite right.

The crowd cheered. The trainer grew angrier. He drew back his whip to lash the ape – a silly thing to do in that crowded audience, but he was beside himself with anger.

Jack saw the movement. He came shooting out of his seat, his young face wrathful. A delirious audience saw a schoolboy pick up the trainer and bounce him down on his rear in the aisle.

The manager really grew nasty. He shouted an order and several burly, roughneck circus hands in dirty white sweaters came running up the aisle. Ajax growled and lumbered to his feet. He came up behind young Jack and the two of them faced the roughnecks. The audience was on its feet now, shouting – but their anger was directed against the circus people. It was an ugly moment. The circus manager, a man who could not be thwarted, had rather lost his head.

The circus toughies came up the aisle with a rush.

And suddenly Jack and Ajax found they had an ally.

A man stepped between them and the circus people. He was tall – a giant of a man, broad-shouldered in a way that told of herculean strength. A fine-looking man with level grey eyes that commanded authority and stopped the rush. It was all so dramatic that, curiously, the audience became quiet though they remained standing, watching intently.

Jack saw him and exclaimed, "Father!"

Ajax saw him and went mad.

The giant ape was hugging the big man, hugging him but gently, his great paws going caressingly over Tarzan's shoulders. And all the time Ajax was talking, talking, saying things in ape-language that meant joy and thankfulness – even though they could not understand what

15

he was saying, everyone there could feel Ajax's frantic delight at meeting Tarzan.

Then the most astonishing thing occurred. From Tarzan's lips came the same guttural sounds. Tarzan was speaking to Ajax in his own language! An enraptured audience stood and watched them. And from the wings a hideously bent figure, his face pock-marked and ravaged with suffering, also watched them, his eyes quite mad with hatred at sight of Tarzan.

"Long have I looked for you, Tarzan," the great ape said.

"Akut, I have thought of you many times," said Tarzan. Akut. Not Ajax – that was Paulvitch's name for the ape. Akut, the king-ape that had been Tarzan's great friend and had accompanied him on one great and dangerous adventure. Tarzan always said that Akut was the most intelligent ape that he had ever met.

The giant man held the great ape in his arms as if in greeting of an old friend. Through his mind was running a train of memories – the jungle, the black Mugambi wielding his deadly knobstick, by his side with bared fangs Sheeta the terrible, Sheeta the savage panther. And by their side Akut and his apes, all friends of Tarzan in that terrible time, all fighting by his side against merciless enemies.

Holding his old ape friend a wave of nostalgia swept over Tarzan. If only he could return to the jungle! But he had a wife and son. The jungle was no place for them. They would die in no time. He had committed his life to England by his act of marriage, but – He sighed. Almost he could smell the scent of the jungle, the alluring odour of primitive Africa.

"I wanted to see you again before I die," said the great ape simply. "I have found you and I am happy. I do not like Tarzan's new jungle – it is not as good as Jungle Island – but I will stay here with you if you want me."

16

"I would like you to stay," said Tarzan, and how true was that statement! "My friend, you could stay with me forever, but this is no land for you."

Tarzan knew it. The ape would be miserable in England's cold winters. It would be wrong to keep him here, however much he would have enjoyed his company. No, England was no place for Akut.

Very gently Tarzan said, "Your home is in Africa. That is where you belong, that is where you will be happiest."

And Akut agreed. He said again, "I do not like your jungle. Now that I have seen you I am content. Now I can return to Jungle Island."

"Now you can return."

At which moment the police arrived, summoned from outside by the manager. The sergeant spoke to Tarzan with respect. "Could you help the manager, sir?" he asked. "The next house is waiting to come in. He says you're holding up the show."

Young Jack broke in then. "I don't think we can be held responsible –"

His father silenced him with a little gesture. He spoke to Akut. "We must leave you for the moment. You must go quietly back with your trainer. I will speak to him tomorrow and make arrangements for you to be taken home."

Akut embraced the mighty Tarzan once again, then quite docilely turned and walked across to the ring, followed by a scowling trainer.

Tarzan spoke to Jack. "Come," he said, and both began to walk up the aisle. Someone began to clap. All at once it was taken up by the entire audience, the applause thundering out. Jack felt mightily proud as he walked up the aisle alongside his giant of a father.

When they were home Jack said, "You spoke to him, dad. How did you learn ape language? How did you know Ajax?"

"Akut," corrected Tarzan. He looked across at his wife.

"You'd better tell him everything," she said with a sigh. This was what she had feared.

So Tarzan briefly told his story. How his father and mother had been marooned on a desert shore in Africa by mutinous seamen.* How he had been born and they had died and he had been brought up by a female ape, wonderful Kala who had lost her own baby. He told of his life of adventure in the forest, of meeting Jack's mother and marrying her there. And he told Jack of an adventure which his son could not remember – how Jack had been kidnapped when he was a baby and taken to Africa by two vicious criminals, Rokoff and Paulvitch, as an act of vengeance on Tarzan. But Tarzan had thwarted them, Rokoff dying in the process and Paulvitch fleeing into the jungle.

Young Jack listened to the story enthralled, hero-worship in his eyes as he gazed at his brilliant father. "Oh, dad, if only I could go to Africa and become an ape-man like you!" he burst out suddenly, and at that Tarzan and his wife exchanged glances.

"That is just what we feared," his mother said. "That is why we never told you of the past, and why we even kept you from zoos and circuses – from African animals. We felt that if ever you knew of your father's adventures it would make you want to go to Africa – and we don't want to lose our only son," she ended softly.

Tarzan's heart sank, looking at his son's bright, intelligent face. He felt the damage had been done. He knew his boy and he knew there was a strong streak of adventure in him. In that moment he knew the call of Africa would be too strong. His heart ached.

Next day Tarzan went to the circus to see Akut. He found that Akut not only had a trainer but an owner, too. He was introduced to a Mr. Michael Sabrov, and he dis-

* *Read Tarzan of the Apes*

18

liked the man on sight. He saw a worn and scarred man, white-haired and lean to the point of emaciation. It was impossible for him to recognize in Sabrov the man he had once known as Alexis Paulvitch.

Tarzan came to the point immediately. "You own Ajax?" Paulvitch nodded. "I would like to buy him."

"Why?"

"I want to send him back to the jungle. That is where he belongs."

Paulvitch said, deliberately, "He is not for sale."

"Name your price," said Tarzan.

"He is not for sale." Paulvitch gloated over the power he had to thwart his old enemy's desires. Tarzan tried his best. He named absurdly high bids for the purchase of Akut, but Paulvitch only shook his head. Finally Tarzan had to return home, his mission a failure.

Next day the circus folded its tent and disappeared. Tarzan tried to trace Akut and its owner, but neither appeared to be with any circus in the land. And then Jack mysteriously disappeared for a few hours.

Jack found where Akut and his owner were staying – in a miserable lodging in London's East End – because the cunning Paulvitch made sure he knew. A man at the circus, paid to look out for the young lad, told him when Jack came as the last of the circus props were being packed.

Jack promptly took train for London. Akut was irresistible. Jack had to see him again. Paulvitch pretended to be friendly and allowed him to sit with Akut in the dingy back room that was Akut's quarters. As yet Paulvitch had no plans but he knew they would form. All he knew was that if he was to get revenge on the man he hated to the point of mania it would be better through his beloved son.

So it was that Jack got into the habit of slipping off to London several days a week, when he was supposed to be studying privately while a new tutor was found for him.

And neither his father nor mother suspected what he was up to.

Akut loved him, as the son of Tarzan. Each time young Jack came to see him he was overjoyed, and for hours they would sit alone together. But Jack wanted to speak the ape language like his father and because Akut was intelligent he appreciated it and most obviously tried to help Jack in his efforts to learn.

It was slow work in the beginning, but then astonishingly Jack realised he was beginning to understand the ape language and after that things went better. In a matter of weeks Jack was able to understand much of what Akut said to him, and could hold a laboured form of conversation with the ape.

All the time the cunning Paulvitch watched and plotted. He could have hurt Tarzan now, through his son, but no plan that his cracked and insane brain devised satisfied him. No plan of revenge would hurt Tarzan as badly as he wanted to hurt him. So he waited, knowing his time would come.

Inevitably Paulvitch was traced by the private detective who was employed by Tarzan to the mean East End lodgings. So one day Paulvitch opened the door and found Tarzan standing outside. Paulvitch was startled, then recovered and invited Tarzan inside.

"I still want to buy Ajax," Tarzan said, giving the name by which Paulvitch knew the ape.

Paulvitch again shook his head, yet thoughts were beginning to race.

"Why do you want him so badly?"

"Ajax is an old friend of mine," Tarzan said. "This is no place for him and I want to return him to Africa where he belongs."

Paulvitch still said no, but an idea was beginning to blossom in his mind. When Tarzan came a third time, Paulvitch pretended to weaken.

"All right, I will sell you Ajax, but only on condition

that I make all arrangements for his sea-voyage to Africa."

That seemed unusual, but Tarzan had to agree to the terms. After all, it did not matter much who made the arrangements so long as Akut was taken safely back to the jungle. He made out a cheque to 'Michael Sabrov', and then asked to see Ajax in order to say goodbye to his old friend. This time Paulvitch permitted it, because by now his twisted brain had thought up a diabolical plan to hurt Tarzan, a way which would hit him harder than any other.

Tarzan smiled at the great ape and said, "I have come to say farewell, my old friend. Who knows, someday I may come back to Africa and we may meet again." But neither believed it – this was to be the parting, both knew.

Giant Akut put his arms round giant Tarzan. "It was worth it, to come all this way just for one more glimpse of my old friend," Akut told him in ape language. "And you have a fine son."

They spoke a little longer, and Tarzan was startled by what Akut told him. When he returned home, having made all arrangements for Akut to be taken aboard ship at Southampton, Tarzan called his son to his study.

Tarzan's face was stern, but the sternness was softened by a twinkle in his grey eyes. "You have been visiting Akut," said Tarzan abruptly.

Jack was startled but would not deny it. He nodded.

"Why didn't you tell me you knew where he was?" Tarzan asked. "You knew I was looking for him."

Jack sighed. He was only a boy, and boys do not always think clearly. "I thought if you found Akut you would immediately send him out of the country. I wanted to get to know him, to make friends with him –"

"– and learn ape language," said Tarzan drily.

"I wanted to be like my father," said Jack softly, and after that Tarzan could not be angry.

"Akut leaves for Africa next Wednesday," Tarzan

said, and at that young Jack leapt to his feet in anguish.

"Oh, dad, must he go? Akut's a fine friend to have. I like him so much, and I am learning such a lot from him."

"He must go," Tarzan told him gently. "Do you think I want to get rid of an old friend, either? This climate is no good for him, and I hate the thought of old Akut being turned into a circus beast. Besides, that owner of his makes me suspicious. There's something about him that puts me on my guard. I can't quite express it, but he seems – well, full of hatred. Akut should not be in his hands."

Tarzan was right, and Jack knew it. And now things began to play into Paulvitch's hands in a way no villain could have planned. Meeting Akut had brought about all that Tarzan and Lady Jane feared. Africa had taken hold of young Jack Clayton. The call *was* irresistible. Nothing on earth would keep Jack out of Africa now, and sitting in his room, thinking about it, Jack thought, "It may as well be now as later. I will go back with Akut."

He came to the decision as simply as that, and immediately began his preparations. He had a small amount of money in the bank and this he drew out. Twice in the days before Akut sailed, Jack went to Paulvitch's lodgings. He told Paulvitch what he planned to do, and Paulvitch's heart leapt at the news, and immediately the last details of his plot of vengeance came to him.

*Paulvitch now knew what he would do and how he would do it to destroy Tarzan's happiness for life.*

Jack had played into the maniac's hands.

On the day of Akut's departure Jack wrote a note for his parents, full of love and affection and telling them not to worry about him. This he posted to give him time to get out of the country.

Then he travelled once again into London, his heart bounding, his nerves tingling. Arriving at the lodgings, Paulvitch let him in. Jack was too excited to notice the man's obvious craziness. Akut was there – though surprisingly Akut was tied by a stout rope to a solid iron ring that had been let into the wall. Akut had never been tied before.

Jack greeted the great ape, then turned because Paulvitch was speaking to him. Paulvitch had a piece of cord in his hands.

"Come here," said Paulvitch. "Put your hands behind your back."

"But why?" asked Jack.

"I want to show you how you can tie Ajax if he gets troublesome on the voyage."

Jack laughed. "Ajax won't be troublesome," he began, but suddenly Paulvitch seemed in a frightful temper.

"Do as I tell you! I will not let you go with Ajax unless I am quite sure you know how to handle him."

Jack shrugged. All right, he would humour the old boy, he thought. He turned his back on the Russian. Deftly Paulvitch secured his arms behind him. And when that was done Paulvitch changed in his manner.

Jack found himself being hurled violently to the ground. In the same movement Paulvitch leapt upon the boy, his fingers clutching for his throat. Jack found himself staring into the face of a man far over the edge into insanity.

Akut reared to his full height and growled his anger. Paulvitch took no heed of him.

"Your father ruined me!" he whispered into Jack's face, so close to his. "I am going to hurt him for that, hurt him in a way he cannot imagine."

Akut was growing frantic, seeing the boy in the grip of the Russian. He roared in fury, and tried to break the rope that held him. It was too strong even for Akut. Again those mighty ape muscles swelled, again Akut tugged and tore at his fastenings. But they held.

"I am going to kill you," Paulvitch gloated. Jack felt the pressure increasing on his throat. "When you are dead I shall mutilate your body. Then I will call your father. He will come in and see you, dead . . . like that.

23

And I will say I left you alone with the ape, and the ape did it."

The pressure increased savagely. Jack was helpless. His head began to swim, his lungs were bursting, the savage fingers at his throat hurting, hurting. . . .

Akut's rage now became awesome. He could see his young friend dying before his eyes. A form of jungle madness came to him, the madness that comes to beasts who are hard-pressed and gives them supernatural strength. Akut hurled himself towards the Russian. There was a cracking sound and the ring came out of the wall.

Paulvitch heard the noise and turned. He saw Akut rearing high above him, saw Death on the face of that terrible ape. It was the last thing he saw. Akut picked him off the body of his young friend, huge hands holding him as if he were a babe. In one second Paulvitch was dead, he would harm no one ever again.

Then the great ape knelt by Jack's side, picking him up in his great hairy arms and crooning to him as if he were a child. Slowly Jack recovered his senses. Then he began to talk to Akut, telling him to untie his bonds. It took him two hours to get Akut to understand and follow his instructions, but finally he was free.

Later that day a young man pushed his old grandmother, veiled and gloved, in a bathchair on to a ship at Southampton. During the voyage the grandmother never left her cabin, and all meals were brought to her there. She had a remarkable appetite for an old lady, the amount of fruit and nuts she consumed being a source of astonishment and comment among the stewards.

When they came to their destination – a small, decaying port on the coast of Africa – the old lady was lowered into a boat and rowed ashore. That was the last they saw of the old lady.

A few hours later ape and boy were in the jungle, Akut gladly shedding his hampering skirts and veil.

And Jack felt that he was a fugitive from mankind,

that events had occurred which meant that he could never return home.

He was only a boy, and his reasoning was faulty. He had never seen death before and Paulvitch's end was terrible. In his young mind was the thought that he was responsible for the death and when the corpse was discovered the authorities would blame him for it. All wrong, of course, but for all his man's strength and stature, Jack was still a naive youngster, shocked by a killing, shaken by his own nearness to death, and incapable of seeing the truth.

He was in the jungle with his great friend, and he felt that here he would have to stay for the rest of his life, far away from policemen and judges and juries. He would have to live as his father had lived.

Perhaps the decision was all the easier for him to make because he wanted to become a jungle man like his great father.

Six years before the events in London, when Paulvitch met a well-merited end, there was another act of vengeance on a man through his child. This time it was a daughter.

It came to Captain Armand Jacot, of the French Foreign Legion. It followed a punitive expedition by the Legion at the end of which a band of Arab cut-throats, bandits and slave-dealers were destroyed, and their leader, Achmet ben Houdin, was a captive in their midst.

To Jacot one day came a deputation led by the father of Achmet. This was the Sheik Amor ben Khatour, a wily man who kept just inside the law.

The sheik spoke of his son – he wanted his release. Captain Jacot shook his head. The sheik spoke on, a mixture of pleading and threats to create disorder if his wishes were not complied with. Captain Jacot remained firm.

Then the sheik made the mistake of trying to bribe this honourable son of France, and at that Jacot drove him out of the camp and called him 'scum' as he did so. The sheik swore to have revenge.

The cut-throat, Achmet ben Houdin, was tried and found guilty and went to his death. A month later little Jeanne Jacot, the seven-year-old daughter of Captain Jacot was kidnapped.

Jacot and his wife were frantic. They had wealth and they offered a reward of enormous proportions. Yet no one came forward to claim it.

True, many sought to enrich themselves, and their bones might be found bleaching in the wastes of Africa. Among those who sought and did not die in their searching, though, were two Swedes, Carl Jenssen and Sven Malbihn.

They were rough men, experienced African travellers, and greedy for money however it could be earned. Wherever they went they were hated and feared by the natives for their cruelty and brutality. For ivory they slaughtered and stole. They were evil men.

One day, five years after the disappearance of Jeanne Jacot, the Swedes encamped outside a native village. The chief came out to them – a thin-faced Arab. Jacot would have recognised him as Sheik ben Khatour.

Jenssen and Malbihn announced they had come to trade for ivory. The Arab shook his head decisively, he had no ivory. It was then that Jenssen noticed a slim figure peering round the doorway of a hut, a young girl. But she was neither Arab nor Negro! The Swede gasped, and nudged his companion. Could it be that after all these years their search was at last to be rewarded?

The Arab noticed their surprise and jerked his head round in the direction of their gaze. A snarl of fury crossed his face as he glimpsed the girl recoiling into the darkness of the hut.

"I have no ivory," he repeated. "I do not wish to trade. Go away. Go now!"

He pushed the two white men from the village, then turned and strode towards the girl. She crouched in terror before him. Viciously he hauled her to her feet and shouted, "Stay inside! Never let strangers see your face. Next time you disobey me I shall have you killed!"

With a blow he hurled her to the ground and left her. She huddled on the dry earth, trying to stifle her moans.

This was all the life she could remember, curses and blows from this Arab who she believed to be her father. Occasionally she dreamed of a different time, and of people who loved her, but these dreams always vanished with a kick or an oath from The Sheik. All her love and affection she lavished upon a repulsive old doll that a slave had made for her. She called this crude wood-carving Geeka and treated it like a child. Now she went to it and kissed and caressed it as she sobbed, "Oh, Geeka, why doesn't my father love me? I try to be good, but all he does is beat me. Oh, Geeka, I wish I was dead."

And so the little girl, who was known in that village as Meriem, cried herself to sleep, hugging the battered doll in her arms as she did so.

In the camp of the Swedes, Jenssen was talking urgently to his companion.

"It was her I tell you," he said. "The Frenchman's daughter. But why hasn't the Arab claimed the reward?"

"Revenge, perhaps," replied Malbihn. "But we could try to buy her from him."

"Not from The Sheik," said Jenssen. "Not if he has kidnapped her out of revenge. But we could always bribe one of his people. The headman, Mbeeda, looked a shifty sort. He would get her for us if we paid him enough."

So they offered Mbeeda a purse of gold to steal the girl away from the Arab. He agreed eagerly and, on the appointed night, they waited silently outside the village gates. Each of them was thinking of the reward offered by Captain Jacot, and spending it in his imagination. Presently they heard a low whistle and a strange native appeared carrying a small sack.

"This is what your gold has bought you," the war-rior said, then he left.

The Swedes looked at each other and then at the sack. Finally Malbihn picked it up and opened it. Inside was the head of the faithless Mbeeda!

Five minutes later the *safari* of Jenssen and Malbihn was travelling rapidly towards the west. Nervous askaris guarded the rear, expecting an attack at any minute. The Sheik was not a man to forget or forgive.

That first night in the jungle remained longest in young Jack's memory. No savage beasts menaced them, no hideous barbarians threatened their night's sleep.

But he had his thoughts, and they were wretched. He thought of his parents' shock when he did not return, their anguish when they received his letter which told them he was responding to the call of Africa.

Jack crouched against the warm hairy body of Akut, high in the branches of a tree, but his thin clothes were little protection against the cold night air and he slept badly. During his hours of wakefulness he thought longingly of his parents, and now, suddenly, he began to doubt the motives which had led him to take flight with Akut.

He was still only a boy, with little experience of the world. He had come all this way and now his thoughts were of going back home, moved by his parents' distress.

An idea came to him in the night. He would head slowly back for civilisation, now that Akut was safely returned to the jungle. He would somehow, one day, return home without anyone knowing. He would see his parents and tell them why he had fled – tell them about Michael Sabrov. They at least would believe him.

His thoughts were jumbled; he had no coherent idea of what he would do when he did see his parents. Boy-like he tried to embrace a plan that satisfied all his requirements. He would have his jungle life for a while and also return to his parents.

But when the sun rose his spirits rose, too. The warm

rays cheered him and the misery of the night was instantly forgotten.

He shook Akut into wakefulness.

"Come," he said. "I am cold and hungry. We will search for food, out there in the sunlight," and he pointed to an open plain, dotted with stunted trees and strewn with jagged rock.

The boy slid to the ground as he spoke, but the ape first looked carefully about, sniffing the morning air. Then satisfied that no danger lurked nearby, he descended slowly to the ground beside the boy.

"Numa and Sabor his mate feast upon those who descend first and look afterwards, while those who look first and descend afterwards live to feast themselves."

Thus the old ape gave the son of Tarzan the boy's first lesson in jungle lore. Side by side they set off across the rough plain. The ape showed him the best places to dig for rodents and worms, but the lad only turned away at the thought of devouring the repulsive things. Some eggs they found, and these he sucked raw. He also ate roots and tubers which Akut unearthed.

Beyond the plain and across a low bluff they came upon water – brackish, ill-smelling stuff in a shallow water-hole, the sides and bottom of which were trampled by the feet of many beasts. A herd of zebra galloped away as they approached.

The lad was too thirsty to reject anything even remotely resembling water, so he drank his fill while Akut stood with raised head, alert for any danger. Before the ape drank he cautioned the boy to be watchful, and as he drank he raised his head from time to time to cast a quick glance towards a clump of bushes a hundred yards away. When he had finished he rose and spoke to the boy in the tongue of the great apes.

"There is no danger near?" he asked.

"None," replied the boy. "I saw nothing move while you drank."

"Your eyes will not help you in the jungle," said

the ape. "Here, if you would live, you must depend upon your ears and nose, but most upon your nose. When we came down to drink and I saw zebras I knew no danger lurked this side of the water-hole, or the zebras would have discovered it and fled before we came.

"But on the other side towards which the wind blows danger might lie concealed. We could not smell it, for its scent is being blown away, and so I bent my ears and eyes down wind where my nose cannot travel."

"And you found – nothing?" asked the lad, with a laugh.

"I found Numa crouching in that clump of bushes where the tall grasses grow," and Akut pointed.

"A lion?" exclaimed the boy. "How do you know? I can see nothing."

"Numa is there, though," replied the great ape. "First I heard him sigh. To you the sigh of Numa may sound no different from the other noises which the wind makes among the grasses and the trees, but later you must learn to know the sigh of Numa.

"Then I watched, and at last I saw the tall grasses moving. See, they are spread there upon either side of Numa's great body, and as he breathes – you see? You see the little motion at either side that is not caused by the wind – the motion none of the other grasses have?"

The boy strained his eyes – better eyes than the ordinary boy inherits – and at last he gave a little exclamation of discovery.

"Yes," he said, "I see. He lies there," and he pointed. "His head is towards us. Is he watching us?"

"Numa is watching us," replied Akut, "but we are in little danger unless we approach too close, for he is lying upon his kill. His belly is almost full, or we would hear him crunching the bones. He is watching us in silence merely from curiosity. Presently he will resume his feeding, or he will rise and come down to the water-hole for a drink.

"Come, we will circle him and catch his scent. The

30

sooner you learn to know it the better, but keep close to the trees as we go around him, for Numa often does what he is least expected to do. And keep your ears and your eyes and your nose open. Remember always there may be an enemy behind every bush, in every tree, and amongst every clump of jungle grass."

Akut set off in a wide circle around the water-hole and the crouching lion. The boy followed close upon his heels, his every sense alert. This was life!

He forgot his resolution of a few hours ago to make his way back to London. He thought now only of the joy of living, and of pitting his wits against the might of the savage jungle beasts which haunted the great untamed continent. He knew no fear. His father had had none to transmit to him.

They were a short distance behind Numa when the boy caught the odour of the carnivore. His face lighted with a smile. Something told him he would have known that scent among a myriad of others even if Akut had not said that a lion lay nearby.

He was, upon the instant, another creature – wary, alert, ready. Thus did the scent of Numa the lion transform the boy into a hunter.

As he trailed Akut he kept an eye cocked over one shoulder in the hope that Numa would rise from his kill and reveal himself. Thus he dropped some little way behind the ape.

Suddenly he heard a shrill scream of warning from Akut. Turning quickly in the direction of his companion, the boy saw standing in his path something which sent tremors of excitement racing through every nerve.

With her body half-merging with a clump of bushes in which she lay was a sleek and beautiful lioness. Her yellow-green eyes were round and staring, boring straight into the eyes of the boy. Not ten paces separated them. Twenty paces behind the lioness stood the great ape, bellowing instructions to the boy and hurling taunts at

31

the lioness to attract her attention from the lad while he gained the shelter of a nearby tree.

But Sabor was not to be diverted. She had her eyes upon the lad. He stood between her and her mate, between her and the kill, and a lioness is short-tempered. Akut's bellowing annoyed her. She uttered a little rumbling growl, taking a step towards the boy.

"The tree!" screamed Akut.

The boy turned and fled, and at the same instant the lioness charged. The tree was only a few paces away. A limb hung ten feet from the ground, and as the boy leapt for it the lioness leapt for him. Like a monkey he pulled himself up and to one side. A great forepaw caught him a glancing blow – just grazing him. One curved talon hooked itself into the waistband of his trousers, ripping them from him as the lioness fell back. Half-naked the lad drew himself to safety as the beast turned and leapt for him once more.

Akut, from a nearby tree, jabbered and scolded, calling the lioness all manner of foul names. The boy imitated the ape and cursed the beast, until seeing the futility of words as weapons he thought of something heavier to hurl. There were only dead twigs and branches at hand, but these he flung at the upturned, snarling face of Sabor just as his father had twenty years ago, when as a boy he too had taunted the great cats of the jungle.

The lioness prowled about the trunk of the tree for a short time, but finally she stalked majestically away and disappeared in the brush that hid her lord, who had not once shown himself during the incident.

Freed from the threat of the lioness, Akut and the boy came to the ground, to take up their interrupted journey once more. The old ape scolded the lad for his carelessness.

"If you had not been so intent upon the lion behind you, you would have discovered the lioness much sooner than you did," he said.

"But you passed right by her without seeing her," retorted the boy.

Akut quickly passed over his own shortcoming.

"It is thus," he said, "that jungle folk die. We go cautiously for a lifetime and then, just for an instant, we forget and –" He ground his teeth in mimicry of the crunching of great jaws in flesh. "It is a lesson," he resumed. "You have learned that you must not for too long keep your eyes, your ears and your nose all bent in the same direction."

That night the son of Tarzan was colder than he had ever been in all his life. His trousers had not been heavy, but they had been much warmer than nothing. And the next day he roasted in the hot sun, for again their way led across wide and treeless plains.

It was still in the boy's mind to travel south and circle back to the coast in search of another outpost of civilization. He said nothing of this plan to Akut, for he knew the old ape would look with displeasure upon any suggestion of separation.

For a month the two wandered on, the boy learning rapidly the laws of the jungle, his muscles adapting themselves to the new mode of life that had been thrust upon them.

The lad found that it came quite naturally to him to swing through the trees. Even at great heights he never felt the slightest dizziness, and when he had caught the knack of the swing and the release he could hurl himself from branch to branch with even greater agility than the heavier Akut.

And with exposure came a toughening of his smooth, white skin, browning now beneath the sun and wind. He had removed his jacket and shirt one day to bathe in a little stream too small to harbour crocodiles. While he and Akut were splashing in the cool water a monkey dropped from the overhanging trees, snatched up the boy's clothing and scampered away with it.

For a time Jack was angry, but when he had been with-

33

out the jacket and shirt for a time he realised that being half clothed was much more uncomfortable than being entirely naked. Soon he did not miss his clothing in the least, and then he came to revel in the freedom of his nakedness.

Occasionally a smile would cross his face as he tried to imagine the surprise of his schoolfriends if they saw him now. They would envy him. How they would envy him! He felt sorry for them at such times, then as he thought of their happiness with their fathers and mothers, a lump would rise in the boy's throat. . . .

He urged Akut onward, for now they were headed westward towards the coast. The old ape thought they were searching for a tribe of his own kind, and the boy did not correct this belief. He would tell Akut his real plans when they came within sight of civilisation.

One day as they were moving slowly beside a river they came unexpectedly upon a native village. Some children were playing in the water. The boy's heart leapt at sight of them – for over a month he had seen no human being. He started towards them, but Akut laid a hand upon his arm to hold him back. The boy shook himself free, however, and with a shout of greeting ran towards the children.

The sound of his voice brought every head erect. Wide eyes stared at him for a moment and then with screams of terror the children ran inside the village gate. Hearing the noise a score of warriors came out with spears and shields in their hands. With menacing shouts and gestures the natives ran towards the threat to their children.

Jack halted when he saw the excitement he had caused. Akut was calling to him to turn and flee, telling him the natives would kill him. Again Jack shouted to them, telling them he came in peace and only wanted to play with their children. They did not understand and believed he wanted to attack them. Angrily they hurled their spears at him.

The boy realised it was hopeless and with a heavy

heart retreated into the jungle. There he found Akut waiting for him in a tree. The ape urged him to come away, for the wise old anthropoid knew they were no match for the skilled warriors who would search for them through the jungle.

Jack agreed and together they swung through the foliage, the ape silent and the boy filled with dismay. His first attempt to make contact with creatures of his own kind had been brutally rejected. He began to feel now that the beasts of the jungle were his only friends.

As they moved through the trees Jack kept looking behind him. He could hear the natives following with shouts and savage cries. Then an idea struck him. He needed clothing and a weapon, and now was an ideal opportunity to obtain them. It would be revenge of a sort too – the warriors would pay for their hostile attitude towards him!

He lagged farther behind until his pursuers were in sight. They did not see him, for they were not looking among the branches of the trees for human quarry. The lad kept just ahead of them.

For a mile the natives continued the search, and then they turned back towards the village. The boy followed them. Akut was no longer in sight, thinking Jack was following. Swinging silently from tree to tree young Tarzan dogged the footsteps of the returning warriors.

At last one of them dropped behind his companions as they followed a narrow path towards the village. A smile lit Jack's face. Swiftly he hurried forward until he moved almost above the unsuspecting native – stalking him as Sheeta the panther stalks his prey.

Suddenly and silently he leapt down upon the broad shoulders of the warrior. The astonished native found steel fingers at his throat and a brawny arm dragging him into the bush. The warrior lay on the ground, expecting each breath to be his last. His spear and shield were wrenched from his hands and his loincloth torn from his waist. Then there was silence.

The native lay still for a while, wondering what had happened and who had attacked him. Then with a low moan he picked himself up and ran back to the village, naked and terrified.

Akut, discovering that Jack had disappeared, turned back to search for him. He had gone only a short distance when he was brought to a sudden and startled halt by the sight of a strange figure moving through the trees. It was Jack.

In his hand was a long spear, down his back hung an oblong shield, while a loincloth was twisted about the youth's middle. A knife was thrust through its folds.

When the boy saw the ape he ran forward to exhibit his trophies. Proudly he called attention to each of his newly won possessions. Boastfully he recounted the details of his exploit.

"I could have killed him with my bare hands," he said, "but I chose to let him live. He will not forget me in a hurry. And now that I have a spear I will show Numa what it means to have me as a foe. Only the white men and the great apes are our friends. We must avoid all the others. I have learnt that much from the jungle."

They made a detour around the village and took up their journey towards the coast. The boy took great pride in his new weapons. He practised continually with the spear, throwing at some object hour by hour as they travelled, until he was accurate and skilful with the weapon. All the time his training in the ways of the jungle went on under the guidance of Akut.

A single spoor was an open book to the keen eyes of the lad. He could distinguish between the innumerable species of herbivora by scent, and he could tell whether an animal was approaching or departing merely by the strength of its odour. Soon he did not need the evidence of his eyes to tell him whether there were two or four lions upwind – a hundred yards away or half-a-mile.

Much of this Akut taught him, but far more was instinctive knowledge – a species of strange intuition in-

36

herited from his father. He had come to love the jungle life. The constant battle of wits against the many deadly foes that lurked by day and by night appealed to the spirit of adventure in him.

So the days passed, and with the travelling, hunting and climbing the boy's muscles developed and his agility increased until even phlegmatic Akut marvelled at the prowess of his pupil. And the boy, realizing his great strength and revelling in it, became careless. He strode through the jungle, his proud head erect, defying danger. Where Akut took to the trees at the first scent of Numa, the lad laughed in the face of the king of beasts and walked boldly past him.

Good fortune was with him for a long time. The lions he met were well-fed or the very boldness of the strange creature so filled them with surprise that thoughts of attack were banished from their minds as they stood, round-eyed, watching his approach and departure. Whatever the reason, on many occasions the boy passed within a few paces of some great lion without arousing more than a warning growl.

But no two lions are alike in character or temper. Because ten lions act similarly under similar conditions one cannot say that the eleventh lion will do likewise – the chances are that he will not.

One day the boy met the eleventh lion. Jack was walking across a small plain upon which grew little clumps of bushes. Akut was a few yards to the left of the lad, who was the first to discover the presence of Numa.

"Run, Akut," called the boy, laughing. "Numa lies hidden in the bushes to my right. Take to the trees, Akut! I, the son of Tarzan, will protect you," and the boy kept straight on towards the brush where Numa lay concealed.

The ape shouted to him to come away, but the lad only flourished his spear and executed an improvised war-dance to show his contempt for the king of beasts. Closer and closer to the dread killer he came until with a sudden, angry growl the lion rose from his bed not ten paces from the youth. A huge fellow he was, this lord of the jungle and the desert. A shaggy mane clothed his shoulders. Cruel fangs armed his great jaws. His yellow-green eyes blazed with hatred and challenge.

The boy, with his pitifully inadequate spear ready in his hand, realized quickly that this lion was different from the others he had met. But he had gone too far now to retreat. The nearest tree lay several yards to his left – the lion would be upon him before he had covered half the distance.

Beyond the lion was a thorn bush – only a few feet beyond him. It was the nearest sanctuary, but Numa stood between it and his prey.

The feel of the long spear shaft in his hand and sight of the bush beyond the lion gave the lad an idea – a preposterous idea – a ridiculous, forlorn hope of an idea.

To the astonishment of Akut and Numa the boy leapt swiftly towards the beast. Just for a second the lion was motionless with surprise, and in that second Jack Clayton put to the crucial test an accomplishment which he had practised at school.

Straight for the savage brute he ran, his spear held butt foremost across his body. Akut shrieked in terror and amazement. The lion stood with wide, round eyes awaiting the attack, ready to rear upon his hind feet and receive this rash creature with blows that could crush the skull of a buffalo.

Just before the lion the boy placed the butt of his spear upon the ground, gave a mighty spring and before the bewildered beast could guess the trick that had been played upon him, sailed over the lion's head into the embrace of the thorn tree – safe but lacerated.

Akut had never before seen a pole-vault. Now he leapt up and down in the safety of his own tree, screaming taunts and boasts at the discomfited Numa, while the boy, torn and bleeding, sought a less uncomfortable position in his thorny retreat. He had saved his life, but at considerable cost in suffering.

It seemed the lion would never leave, and it was a full hour before the angry brute gave up his vigil and strode majestically away across the plain. When he was at a safe distance the boy extricated himself from the thorn tree, but not without inflicting new wounds upon his already tortured flesh.

It was many days before the outward evidence left him of the lesson he had learned, while the impression upon his mind remained with him for life. Never again did he uselessly tempt fate.

For several days the boy and the ape lay up while the former recovered from the painful injuries inflicted by the sharp thorns. The great anthropoid licked the wounds of his human friend and they soon healed, for healthy flesh quickly replaces itself.

When the lad felt fit again the two continued their journey towards the coast, and once more the boy's mind was filled with pleasurable anticipation.

And at last the much-dreamed-of moment came. They were passing through a tangled forest when the boy's sharp eyes discovered an old but well-marked spoor – a spoor that set his heart leaping – the spoor of man, of white men. For among the prints of naked feet were the well-defined outlines of European-made boots. The trail, which marked the passage of a good-sized company, pointed north at right angles to the course the boy and the ape were taking towards the coast.

Doubtless these white men knew the nearest coast settlement. They might even now be headed for it. At any rate, it would be worthwhile overtaking them, if only for the pleasure of meeting again creatures of his own kind. The lad was all excitement, eager to be off in pursuit.

Akut disagreed. He wanted nothing of men. To him the lad was a fellow-ape, for he was the son of the king of apes. He tried to dissuade the boy, telling him that

39

soon they would come upon a tribe of their own folk, where the boy would be king as his father had been before him.

But Jack was obdurate. He insisted he wanted to see white men again. He wanted to send a message to his parents. Akut listened, and as he listened the intuition of the beast suggested the truth to him – the boy was planning to return to his own kind.

The thought filled the old ape with sorrow. He loved the boy as he had loved the father, with the loyalty and faithfulness of a hound for its master. In his ape brain and his ape heart he had nursed the hope that he and the lad would never be separated. He saw all his fondly cherished plans fading away, and yet he remained loyal to the lad and to his wishes. Though disconsolate, he gave in to the boy's determination to pursue the *safari* of the white men, accompanying him upon what he believed would be their last journey together.

The spoor was only a couple of days old when the two discovered it, which meant that the slow-moving caravan was only a few hours distant. The boy was in the lead, excitement and anticipation driving him ahead of his companion. And it was the boy who first saw the rearguard of the caravan and the white men he had been so anxious to overtake.

Stumbling along the tangled trail were a dozen heavily laden natives who, from fatigue or sickness, had dropped behind. They were being prodded by the black soldiers of the rearguard, kicked when they fell, and then roughly jerked to their feet and hustled onward. On either side walked a giant white man, heavy blond beards almost obliterating their faces.

The boy's lips formed a glad cry of greeting, a cry that was never uttered. For almost immediately he saw that both the white men were wielding heavy whips brutally upon the naked backs of poor devils staggering beneath loads that would have overtaxed the strength of strong men at the beginning of a new day.

Every now and then the rearguard and the white men cast apprehensive glances rearward, as though expecting danger from that quarter. The boy had paused after his first sight of the caravan, and now was following slowly in the wake of the brutal spectacle.

Presently Akut came up with him. To the ape there was less horror in the sight than to the lad, yet even the great ape growled beneath his breath at the useless torture being inflicted upon the helpless slaves. He looked at the boy. Now that he had caught up with the creatures of his own kind, why did he not rush forward and greet them? He put the question to his companion.

"They are fiends," muttered the boy. "I could not travel with them. If I did I would set upon them and kill them the first time they beat their people as they are beating them now. But," he added, after a moment's thought, "I can ask them the whereabouts of the nearest port and then, Akut, we can leave them."

The ape made no reply, and the boy swung to the ground and started at a brisk walk towards the *safari*. He was a hundred yards away when one of the whites caught sight of him. The man gave a shout of alarm, instantly levelling his rifle at the boy and firing. The bullet struck just in front of its mark, scattering turf and fallen leaves against the lad's legs. A second later the other white and black soldiers of the rearguard were firing hysterically at the boy.

Jack leapt behind a tree, unhit. Days of panic-ridden flight through the jungle had filled Carl Jenssen and Sven Malbihn with jangling nerves and their native boys with unreasoning terror. Every new note from behind sounded to their frightened ears like the coming of The Sheik and his bloodthirsty band.

They were in a blue funk, and sight of the naked white warrior stepping silently out of the jungle had been sufficient shock to let loose in action all the pent up nerve energy of Malbihn, who had been the first to see the

41

strange apparition. And Malbihn's shout and shot had set the others going.

When their first fright had spent itself, and they came to take stock of what they had been fighting, it developed that Malbihn alone had seen anything clearly. Several of the boys claimed they too had obtained a good view of the creature, but their descriptions of it varied so greatly that Jenssen, who had seen nothing himself, was inclined to be a trifle sceptical. One of the bearers insisted that the thing had been eleven feet tall, with a man's body and the head of an elephant!

When, after conquering their nervousness, the rear-guard advanced to investigate they found nothing, for Akut and the boy had retreated out of range of the unfriendly guns.

Jack was disheartened and upset.

"The lesser beasts flee from me in terror," he murmured, half to himself. "The greater beasts are ready to tear me to pieces at sight. Black men would kill me with their spears or arrows. And now white men, men of my own kind, have fired upon me and driven me away. Are all the creatures of the world my enemies?"

The old ape drew closer to the boy.

"There are the great apes," he said. "They will be the friends of Akut's friend. Let us go now and continue our search for the great apes – our people."

A year had passed since the two Swedes were driven in terror from the savage country where The Sheik held sway. Meriem still played with Geeka lavishing all her childish love on the doll. She was too old to play with dolls. In a few years she would be married off to one of The Sheik's kinsmen, but only in Geeka could she find the gentleness she wanted. Everyone else in the village treated her with contempt and hatred.

One day Meriem was sitting at the foot of a large tree which grew inside the palisade close to the edge of the village. She was making a tent of leaves for Geeka. Meriem was totally absorbed in play – so much so that she did not notice the gentle swaying of the branches above her as they bent to the body of the creature who had entered them stealthily from the jungle.

In happy ignorance the girl played on while from above two steady eyes looked down upon her – unblinking, unwavering. There was only Meriem in this part of the village which had been almost deserted since The Sheik left long months before upon his journey to the north.

And out in the jungle, an hour's march from the village, The Sheik was leading his returning caravan homeward.


It was nearly a year since the white men had fired upon the lad and driven him back into the jungle. A year that had done much for the boy – turning his already mighty muscles into thews of steel, and developing his woodcraft to a point where it verged upon the uncanny.

He became at last a creature of marvellous physical powers and mental cunning. He was still a boy, yet so great was his strength that the powerful anthropoid with whom he often wrestled was no match for him.

As the two searched for a band of the almost extinct species of ape to which Akut belonged they lived upon the best that the jungle afforded. Antelope and zebra fell to the boy's spear or were dragged down by the two powerful beasts of prey.

Always they were searching for the elusive anthropoids who were to welcome them with open arms. And at last they found them. Deep in the jungle, buried far from sight of man they came upon a little natural arena like that which had witnessed the wild ceremony of the Dum-Dum long years before.

First, at a great distance, they heard the beating of the drum of the great apes. They were sleeping in the safety of a huge tree when the booming sound disturbed them. Both awoke at once. Akut was the first to interpret the strange rhythms.

"The great apes!" he growled. "They dance the Dum-Dum. Come, Korak, son of Tarzan, let us go to our people."

Months before, Akut had given the boy a name of his own choosing, since he could not master the man-given name of Jack. Korak is as near as it can be interpreted into human speech. In the language of the apes it means Killer. Now Korak rose upon the branch of the great tree where he had been sleeping. He stretched his lithe young muscles, the moonlight filtering through the foliage and dappling his brown skin with little patches of light.

The ape too stood up, half squatting after the manner of his kind. Low growls rumbled from the bottom of his deep chest – growls of excited anticipation. The boy growled in harmony with the ape. Then the anthropoid slid softly to the ground. Close by, in the direction of the booming drum, lay a clearing which they must cross. The moon flooded it with silvery light. Half erect, the great ape shuffled into the full glare of the moon.

At his side, swinging gracefully along in marked contrast to his companion, strode the boy, the dark, shaggy coat of one brushing against the smooth, clear hide of the other.

Louder and louder came the beating of the drum. Now at last they could hear the growling of the dancing apes, and strong to their nostrils came the scent of their kind. The lad trembled with excitement. The hair down Akut's spine stiffened.

Silently they crept through the jungle as they neared the meeting-place of the apes. Presently through a break in the foliage the scene burst upon the eager eyes of the boy. To Akut it was familiar, but to Korak it was all new. His nerves tingled at the savage sight. The great bulls were dancing in the moonlight, leaping in a circle

44

about the flat-topped earthen drum around which three old females sat beating its resounding top with sticks worn smooth by long years of use.

Akut, knowing the temper of his kind, was too wise to make their presence known until the frenzy of the dance had passed. After the drum was quiet and the bellies of the tribe well filled he would hail them. Then would come a parley, after which he and Korak would be accepted into membership by the community. There might be those who would object, but these could be overcome by brute force.

As the moon declined slowly towards the horizon the booming of the drum decreased. At last the final note was struck and the huge beasts turned to fall upon the feast they had dragged there for the orgy.

Akut explained to Korak that the rites celebrated the choosing of a new king, and he pointed out the massive figure of the shaggy monarch.

When the apes had filled their bellies and many of them had sought the trees to curl up in sleep Akut plucked Korak by the arm.

"Come," he whispered.

He advanced slowly through the trees until he stood upon a bough overhanging one side of the amphitheatre. Here he waited in silence for a moment. Then he uttered a low growl. Instantly a score of apes leapt to their feet. Their savage little eyes sped quickly around the edge of the clearing.

The king ape was the first to see the two figures upon the branch. He gave voice to an ominous growl. Then he took a few lumbering steps in the direction of the intruders. His hair was bristling. His legs were stiff, giving a halting, jerky motion to his gait. Behind him pressed a number of bulls.

He stopped before he came beneath the two – just far enough to be beyond their spring. Here he stood rocking himself to and fro upon his short legs, baring his fangs and rumbling an ever-increasing volume of growls.

Akut knew he was working himself up to a proper pitch of rage to warrant an attack upon them. The old ape did not wish to fight. He had come with the boy to cast in his lot with the tribe.

"I am Akut," he said. "This is Korak. Korak is the son of Tarzan who was king of the apes. I too was king of the apes who dwelt in the midst of the great waters. We have come to hunt with you, to fight with you. We are great hunters. We are mighty fighters. Let us come in peace."

The king ceased his rocking. He eyed the pair from beneath his beetling brows. His bloodshot eyes were savage and crafty. His kingship was very new and he was jealous of it. He feared the intrusion of two strange apes. The sleek, brown, hairless body of the lad spelled man, and man he feared and hated.

"Go away!" he growled. "Go away, or I will kill you."

The eager boy standing behind the great Akut was trembling with anticipation and happiness. He wanted to leap down among those hairy monsters and show them he was their friend. He had expected them to receive him with open arms, and now the words of the king ape filled him with indignation and anger.

The ape was almost directly beneath him. Before Akut could guess his intention the boy leapt to the ground directly in the path of the king.

"I am Korak!" shouted the boy. "I came to live among you as a friend. You want to drive me away. Very well then, I shall go. But before I go I shall show you that the son of Tarzan is your master, as his father was before him – that he is not afraid of your king or you."

For an instant the king ape stood motionless with surprise. Akut was equally astonished. Now he shouted excitedly for Korak to come back. He knew that in the sacred arena the other bulls would come to the aid of their ruler against an outsider. Once their savage strength was added to the battle the end would come quickly.

46

To leap to the boy's rescue would mean death for Akut too, but the brave old ape never hesitated. Bristling and growling, he dropped to the ground just as the king ape charged.

The beast's hands clutched for their hold as he sprang upon the lad. The fierce jaws were widely distended to bury the yellow fangs deep in the brown hide. Korak too leapt forward to meet the attack, but leapt crouching beneath the outstretched arms.

At the instant of contact the lad pivoted on one foot, and with all the weight of his body and the strength of his trained muscles drove a clenched fist into the bull's stomach. With a gasp the king ape collapsed, clutching futilely for the agile, naked creature nimbly sidestepping from his grasp.

Howls of rage broke from the bull apes as with murder in their savage hearts they rushed forward upon Korak and Akut. But the old ape was too wise to court any such unequal encounter. To have counselled the boy to retreat now would have been useless and Akut knew it. To delay even a second in argument would have sealed the death-warrants of them both.

There was only a single hope and Akut seized it. Grasping the lad round the waist he lifted him bodily from the ground, and turning ran swiftly towards another tree which swung low branches above the arena. Close upon their heels swarmed the hideous mob. But Akut, old though he was and burdened by the weight of the struggling Korak, was still fleeter than his pursuers.

With a bound he grasped a low limb and swung himself and the boy to temporary safety. He did not hesitate there but raced on through the jungle night, bearing his burden to safety. For a time the bulls pursued, but after a while they abandoned the chase, standing roaring and screaming until the jungle reverberated to their hideous noises. Then they turned and retraced their way to the amphitheatre.

## Korak Rescues a Girl

It was an unhappy Korak who wandered aimlessly through the jungle the day after his inhospitable reception by the great apes. His heart was heavy with disappointment. Unsatisfied vengeance smouldered in his breast. He looked with hatred upon the denizens of his jungle world, baring his fighting fangs and growling at those who came within range of his senses.

They were moving downwind, slowly and warily, because the advantage was with whatever beast might be hunting ahead of them. Suddenly the two halted simultaneously. Like creatures hewn from solid rock they stood immovable, listening. Not a muscle quivered. For several seconds they remained thus, then Korak advanced cautiously a few yards and leaped nimbly into a tree. Akut followed close upon his heels. Neither had made a noise that would have been audible to human ears at a dozen paces.

Stopping often to listen they crept forward through the trees.

Finally the lad caught a glimpse of a palisade a hundred yards ahead, and beyond it the tops of some goatskin tents and a number of thatched huts. His lip curled in a savage snarl. He signed to Akut to remain where he was while he advanced to reconnoitre.

Slinking through the lower branches of the trees, leaping lightly from one jungle giant to its neighbour, or swinging from one handhold to another Korak came silently towards the village. He heard a voice beyond the palisade and towards that he made his way.

A great tree overhung the enclosure at the very point from which the voice came. Into this Korak crept. His spear was ready in his hand. His ears told him of the proximity of a human being.

With raised spear he crept among the branches of the tree, glaring downward in search of the owner of the voice. At last he saw a human back. The spear hand flew to the throwing position. And then Korak paused. He leaned forward to get a better view of the target. Astonished, he saw her.

Now he lowered his spear cautiously so that it would make no noise against foliage or branches. Quietly he crouched in a comfortable position along a great limb, and there he lay with wide eyes looking down in wonder upon the creature he had crept upon to kill – looking down on a girl, a nut-brown maiden!

Korak wondered what the girl would do if he dropped suddenly from the tree to her side. Most likely she would scream and run away. Then the men of the village would come with spears and guns and set upon him. They would either kill him or drive him away.

A lump rose in the boy's throat. He craved the companionship of his own kind, though he scarcely realized how greatly. He would have liked to slip down beside the girl and talk with her, though he knew from the words he had overheard that she spoke a language with which he was unfamiliar.

At last he hit upon a plan. He would attract her attention, and reassure her by a smiling greeting from a greater distance. Silently he wormed his way back into the tree.

He had scarcely left his position when his attention was attracted by a considerable noise upon the opposite side of the village. By moving a little he could see the gate at the far end of the main street. A number of men, women, and children were running towards it. It swung open, revealing the head of a caravan upon the opposite side.

In trooped the motley organization – black slaves and dark-hued Arabs of the northern deserts, cursing camel-drivers urging on their vicious charges, overburdened donkeys enduring with stoic patience the brutalities of their masters, goats, sheep, and horses. Into the village they all trooped behind a tall, sour, old man, who rode without greeting those who shrank from his path directly to a large goatskin tent in the centre of the village. Here he spoke to a wrinkled hag.

Korak, from his vantage spot, could see it all. He saw the old man asking questions of the black woman, and then he saw her point towards a secluded corner of the village, in the direction of the tree beneath which the girl played. This must be her father, thought Korak. He had been away, and his first thought upon returning was of his daughter. How glad she would be to see him! Korak sighed. He thought of his own father and mother far away in London.

He returned to his place in the tree above the girl. If he couldn't have happiness of this sort himself he wanted to enjoy the happiness of others.

The Arab was striding softly towards the girl. In a moment he would be beside her, and then how surprised and delighted she would be! Korak's eyes sparkled in anticipation – and now the old man stood behind the girl. His stern old face was still unrelaxed. The girl was still unconscious of his presence. She prattled on to the unresponsive Geeka. Then the old man coughed.

With a start the girl glanced quickly over her shoulder. Korak could see her full face now.

He could see her great dark eyes. He looked for the happy smile that would follow recognition, but it did not come. Instead terror, stark, paralysing terror, was mirrored there, in the expression of her mouth, in the tense, cowering attitude of her body. A grim smile curved the thin, cruel lip of the Arab. The girl started to crawl away, but before she could get out of his reach the old man kicked her brutally, sending her sprawling upon the grass.

Above them, in the tree, a beast crouched where a

moment before had been a boy – a beast with dilating nostrils and bared fangs – a beast that trembled with rage.

The Sheik was stooping to reach for the girl when Korak dropped to the ground at his side. His spear was still in his hand but he had forgotten it. Instead, his right hand was clenched, and as The Sheik took a backward step, astonished by this strange apparition, a heavy fist landed full upon his mouth.

Bleeding and senseless, The Sheik sank to earth. Korak turned towards the girl. She had regained her feet and stood, wide-eyed and frightened, looking first into his face and then, horrorstruck, at the unconscious figure of The Sheik. In an involuntary gesture of protection the boy threw an arm around the girl's shoulders and stood waiting for the Arab to regain consciousness. For a moment they remained thus, then the girl spoke.

"When he regains his senses he will kill me," she said in Arabic.

Korak could not understand her. He shook his head, speaking first in English and then in the language of the great apes, but neither of these was intelligible to her. She leaned forward and touched the hilt of the long knife that the Arab wore. Then she raised her hand above her head and drove an imaginary blade into her breast. Korak understood.

"Come," he said. "The jungle is kinder than man. You shall live in the jungle and Korak and Akut will protect you."

She did not understand his words, but the pressure of his arm drawing her away from the prostrate Arab and the tents was quite intelligible. One shapely arm crept about his waist and together they walked towards the palisade.

Beneath the great tree that had harboured Korak he lifted her in his arms and leapt nimbly into the lower branches. Her arms were around his neck and from one

51

small hand Geeka dangled down his straight young back.

The two had gone only a short distance from the village when the girl spied the huge proportions of the great Akut. With a half-stifled scream she clung more closely to Korak, and pointed fearfully towards the ape.

Akut, thinking that the lad was returning with a prisoner, came growling towards them – a girl aroused no more sympathy in the beast's heart than would a full-grown bull ape. She was a stranger and therefore to be killed. He bared his yellow fangs as he approached, but to his surprise Korak bared his likewise.

"Ah," thought Akut, "The Killer has taken a mate."

So, obedient to the tribal laws of his kind, he left them alone, becoming suddenly absorbed in a fuzzy caterpillar of peculiarly succulent appearance. The larva disposed of, he glanced from the corner of an eye at Korak. The youth had placed his burden upon a large limb, where she clung desperately to keep from falling.

"She will accompany us," said Korak to Akut, jerking a thumb in the direction of the girl. "Do not harm her. We will protect her."

Akut shrugged. To be burdened by the young of man was not to his liking. He could see from her evident fright at her position on the branch, and from the terrified glances she cast in his direction that she was hopelessly unfit. By all the ethics of Akut's training and inheritance the unfit should be eliminated. But if Korak wanted this she there was nothing to be done about it but to tolerate her.

Akut sighed. Then he rose, expanded his great chest, and strutted back and forth along a substantial branch, for even a puny thing like this she of Korak's could admire his fine coat and graceful carriage.

But poor Meriem only shrank closer to Korak and almost wished that she were back in the village of The Sheik.

The hideous ape frightened her. He was so large and so ferocious in appearance. She could not know of the bond of fellowship which existed between this great brute and the godlike youth who had rescued her from The Sheik.

Meriem spent an evening and a night of appalling terror. Korak and Akut led her along dizzy ways as they searched for food. Once they hid her in the branches of a tree while they stalked a nearby buck. Even her natural terror of being left alone in the awful jungle was submerged in a greater horror as she saw the man and the beast spring simultaneously upon their prey and drag it down; as she saw the handsome face of her preserver contorted in a bestial snarl; as she saw his strong, white teeth buried in the soft flesh of the kill.

When he came back to her, blood smeared his face, hands and breast, and she shrank from him as he offered her a huge hunk of hot, raw meat. He was disturbed by her refusal to eat and swung away into the forest to return with fruit for her. This time she did not shrink away but acknowledged his gift with a smile that was more than ample payment to the affection-starved boy.

The sleeping problem vexed Korak. He knew the girl could not balance herself in safety in a tree crotch while she slept, nor would it be safe to permit her to sleep on the ground open to the attacks of prowling beasts of prey. There was only one solution – he must hold her in his arms all night. And that he did, with Akut braced on one side of her and he on the other, so that she was warmed by the bodies of them both.

She did not sleep much until the night was half spent, but at last Nature overcame her terrors of the black abyss beneath and the wild beast at her side, and she fell into a deep slumber.

When she opened her eyes the sun was well up. At first she could not believe in the reality of her position. Her head had rolled from Korak's shoulder, so that her eyes were directed upon the hairy back of the ape. At

sight of it she shrank away. Then she realized that someone was holding her, and turning her head she saw the
smiling eyes of the youth.

When he smiled she could not fear him, and now she
shrank closer against him in natural revulsion of the
rough coat of the brute upon her other side.

Korak spoke to her in the language of the apes, but
she shook her head and replied in Arabic, which was
as unintelligible to him as was ape speech to her.

Akut sat up and looked at them. He could understand what Korak said, but the girl made only foolish
noises that were entirely unintelligible and ridiculous.
Akut could not understand what Korak saw in her to
attract him. He looked at her steadily, appraising her
carefully, then he scratched his head, rose, and shook
himself.

His movement gave the girl a little start – she had forgotten Akut for the moment. Again she shrank from
him. The beast saw that she feared him, and being a
brute enjoyed the terror his brutishness inspired.
Crouching, he extended his huge hand stealthily towards
her, as though to seize her. She shrank still farther away.

Akut's eyes were busy drinking in the humour of the
situation – he did not see the narrowing eyes of the boy
upon him.

As the ape's fingers were about to close upon the girl's
arm the youth rose suddenly with a short, vicious growl.
A clenched fist flew before Meriem's eyes to land full
upon the snout of the astonished Akut. With an explo-
sive bellow the anthropoid reeled backward and tumbled from the tree.

Korak stood glaring down at him when a sudden
swish in the bushes close by attracted his attention. The
girl too was looking down, but she saw nothing except
the angry ape scrambling to his feet. Then, like a bolt
from a crossbow, a mass of spotted, yellow fur shot into
view straight for Akut's back. It was Sheeta, the leopard.

# Meriem the Jungle Girl

As the leopard leaped for the great ape Meriem gasped in surprise and horror. For scarcely had the carnivore burst into view before the youth had leapt far out above him, so that as Sheeta was almost sinking her fangs and talons in Akut's broad back Korak landed full upon the leopard's shoulders.

The cat halted in mid-air, missed the ape by a hair's breadth, and with savage snarlings rolled over on its back, clutching and clawing in an effort to dislodge the antagonist biting at its neck and knifing it in the side.

Akut, startled by the sudden rush from his rear, was in the tree beside the girl with an agility little short of marvellous in so heavy a beast. But sight of what was going on below brought him as quickly to the ground again. Personal differences were quickly forgotten in the danger which menaced his human companion.

The result was that Sheeta found two ferocious creatures fighting him. Shrieking, snarling and growling, the three rolled hither and thither among the underbrush.

But it was the boy's knife which eventually decided the battle, and the fierce feline suddenly shuddered convulsively and rolled over upon its side. The youth and the ape rose and faced one another across the carcass. Korak jerked his head in the direction of the girl in the tree.

"Leave her alone," he said. "She is mine."

Akut grunted, blinked his bloodshot eyes, and turned towards the body of Sheeta. Standing erect upon it he threw out his great chest and gave voice to so horrid a scream that once again the girl shuddered and shrank back. It was the victory cry of the bull ape that has made a kill.

The boy only looked on for a moment in silence, then he leapt into the tree again to the girl's side. Akut presently rejoined them. For a few minutes he busied himself licking his wounds, then he wandered off to hunt his breakfast.

For month after month the strange life of the three continued. To the ape and Korak it was a dull time, unmarked by any unusual events. To the young girl it was a constant nightmare of horror, though gradually she grew accustomed to looking death unblinkingly in the face. Then she too began to learn the language of the apes, and Akut and Korak were able to teach her jungle craft until she could take part in the chase and act as lookout.

Korak built a little shelter for her, high among the swaying branches of a giant tree. There Meriem slept in comfort and safety while the ape and the boy perched nearby, protecting her against any possible danger.

After they had built the shelter, the three did not range so widely during the day, for they had always to return to their tree at night. Life fell into a pattern – the searching for food and the sleeping with full bellies. Korak no longer thought of returning to civilisation, since in Meriem he had found what he most needed – human companionship.

Meriem, for her part, idolised the boy and saw in him everything that was good and brave. For her too the jungle became a home, a sanctuary where she found friendship, trust, and love.

Geeka, that symbol of an unhappy past, had been transformed. Her dress was now identical to Meriem's, a leopardskin loincloth and the bright feathers of a parrakeet in her hair.

One day the doll sat against the trunk of a tree, while her mistress stretched out along a branch and talked to her.

"Well, Geeka," she said, "our Korak has been gone a long time today. The jungle is empty without him.

There is no excitement, no adventure, when he and Akut are away."

Suddenly Meriem's one-sided conversation was interrupted by one of her little monkey friends, who landed with a flying leap on her shoulder.

"Climb!" he cried. "Climb! The Mangani are coming."

Meriem glanced lazily over her shoulder at the excited animal.

"Climb yourself, little Manu," she said. "The only Mangani in our jungle are Korak and Akut. It is they you have seen returning from the hunt. Some day you will see your own shadow, little Manu, and then you will be frightened to death."

But the monkey only screamed his warning more lustily, before he raced upward towards the safety of the high terrace where Mangani, the great ape, could not follow. Presently Meriem heard the sound of approaching bodies swinging through the trees. She listened attentively. There were two, and they were great apes — Korak and Akut.

Meriem decided that she would pretend to be asleep and play a joke on Korak. So she lay very still, with eyes tightly closed. She heard the two approaching closer and closer. They were in the adjoining tree now and must have discovered her, for they had halted. Why were they so quiet? Why did not Korak call out his usual greeting?

The quietness was ominous. It was followed presently by a very stealthy sound — one of them was creeping upon her. Was Korak planning a joke upon his own account? Cautiously she opened her eyes, and as she did so her heart stood still. Creeping silently towards her was a huge bull ape that she had never seen before. Behind was another like him.

With the agility of a squirrel Meriem was on her feet, and at the same instant the great bull lunged for her. Leaping from limb to limb the girl fled through the

57

jungle, while close behind came the two great apes.

From tree to tree swung Meriem, always working upward towards the smaller branches which would not bear the weight of her pursuers. Faster and faster came the bull apes after her. The clutching fingers of the foremost were almost upon her again and again, but she eluded them by sudden bursts of speed or reckless chances as she threw herself across dizzy spaces.

Slowly she was gaining her way to the greater heights where safety lay when, after a particularly daring leap, the swaying branch she grasped bent low beneath her weight.

Meriem had misjudged the strength of the limb. It gave slowly at first. Then there was a tearing sound as it parted from the trunk.

Releasing her hold, Meriem dropped among the foliage beneath, clutching for a new support. She found it a dozen feet below the broken limb.

But scarcely had she scrambled to a place of safety before the body of the huge ape dropped at her side and a great hairy arm went about her waist.

Almost at once the other ape reached his companion's side. He made a lunge at Meriem, but her captor swung her away, bared his fighting fangs, and growled ominously. Meriem struggled to escape. She struck at the hairy breast and bearded cheek. She fastened her strong white teeth in one shaggy forearm. The ape cuffed her viciously across the face, then turned to his fellow, who desired the prize for his own.

The captor dropped quickly to the ground beneath. The other ape followed him and here they fought, occasionally abandoning their duel to pursue and recapture the girl, who took every opportunity to escape. But always they overtook her, and first one and then the other possessed her as they struggled to tear one another to pieces for the prize.

Often the girl came in for blows that were intended for a hairy foe. Once she was felled, lying unconscious while the apes tore into one another in fierce and terrible combat.

The larger bull was slowly tearing his antagonist to pieces. They rolled upon the ground biting and striking. Again, erect upon their hind legs they pulled and tugged like human wrestlers. But always the giant fangs found their bloody part to play until both combatants and the ground around were red with gore.

Meriem, through it all, lay unconscious on the ground. At last one found a hold upon the jugular of the other and they went down for the last time.

It was the larger bull who rose alone from that last embrace. He shook himself. A deep growl rumbled from his hairy throat. He waddled back and forth between the body of the girl and that of his vanquished foe. Then he stood upon the latter and gave tongue to his hideous challenge.

The great ape waddled once more to the girl's side. He turned her over upon her back and, stooping, began to sniff her face and breast. She lived. The monkeys were returning. They came in swarms, and from above hurled down insults upon the victor.

The ape showed his displeasure by baring his teeth and growling up at them. Then he stooped, and lifting the girl to his shoulder stalked off through the jungle. In his wake followed the angry mob.

## Korak to the Rescue

Korak, returning from the hunt, heard the jabbering of the excited monkeys. He knew that something was seriously wrong. Histah the snake had probably coiled his folds about some careless Manu.

The youth hurried on ahead. The monkeys were Meriem's friends. He would help them if he could. He travelled rapidly along the middle terrace. In the tree

59

by Meriem's shelter he deposited his trophies of the hunt and called aloud to her. There was no answer. He dropped quickly to a lower level. She might be hiding from him.

Upon a great branch where Meriem often swung he saw Geeka propped against the tree trunk. What could it mean? Meriem had never left Geeka alone before. Korak picked up the doll and tucked it in his belt. He called again, more loudly, but no Meriem answered his summons. In the distance the jabbering of the excited Manus was growing less distinct.

Could their excitement be in any way connected with Meriem's disappearance? The bare thought was enough. Without waiting for Akut, Korak swung rapidly in the direction of the chattering mob. A few minutes was enough to overtake the rearmost. At sight of him they started screaming and pointing downward ahead of them, and a moment later Korak saw the cause of their rage.

The youth's heart stood still in terror as he saw the limp body of the girl across the hairy shoulders of a great ape.

A groan escaped his lips, then he dropped plummet-like in mad descent towards the perpetrator of this hideous crime.

The bull ape turned at the first note of this new and menacing voice, and as he turned Korak's rage increased. For he saw that the creature before him was none other than the king ape who had driven him away from the great anthropoids.

Dropping the body of the girl to the ground the bull turned to battle anew for possession of his prize, but this time he looked for an easy conquest. He too recognized Korak. Had he not chased him away from the amphitheatre without even having to lay fang or paw upon him. With lowered head and bulging shoulders he rushed headlong for the smooth-skinned creature who was daring to question his right to his prey.

They met head on like two charging bulls, to go down together tearing and striking. Korak forgot his knife. Rage and bloodlust such as his could only be satisfied by the feel of flesh between rending fangs, by the gush of new life-blood against his bare skin. For though he did not realize it, Korak was fighting for something more compelling than hate or revenge – he was a great male fighting another male for a she of his own kind.

So impetuous was the attack of the man-ape that he found his hold before the anthropoid could prevent him – a savage hold, with strong jaws closed upon a pulsing jugular. There he clung with closed eyes, while his fingers sought another hold upon the shaggy throat.

It was then that Meriem opened her eyes. At the sight before her they went wide.

"Korak!" she cried. "Korak! My Korak! I knew you would come. Kill him, Korak! Kill him!" And with flashing eyes and heaving bosom the girl ran to Korak's side to encourage him. Near by lay his spear, where he had flung it as he charged the ape. The girl saw it and snatched it up.

She was excited, but cool and entirely unafraid. Her Korak was battling with another Mangani who would have stolen her, but she did not seek the safety of an overhanging bough to watch the battle from afar. Instead she placed the point of Korak's spear against the bull ape's side and plunged the sharp point deep into the savage heart. Korak had not needed her aid, for the great bull had already been as good as dead, with the blood gushing from his torn jugular. But Korak rose smiling with a word of thanks for his helper.

How tall and fine she was! Had she changed suddenly within the few hours of his absence, or had his battle with the ape affected his vision? His glance rose to Meriem's face and a slow flush suffused his own. Now, indeed, was he looking upon her through new eyes – the eyes of a man looking upon a maid.

And Meriem? She was a woman. Always she had

loved Korak. In all the jungle there was no other creature so strong, so handsome, or so brave.

Korak came close to her.

"Meriem," he whispered, and his voice was husky as
he laid a brown hand upon her bare shoulder.
"Meriem!"

Suddenly he crushed her to him. She looked up into
his face, laughing, and then he bent and kissed her full
upon the mouth.

Even then she did not understand. She did not recall
ever having been kissed before. It was very nice. Meriem
liked it. She thought it was Korak's way of showing
how glad he was that the great ape had not succeeded in
running away with her.

She was glad too, so she put her arms around Korak's
neck and kissed him again and again. Then, discovering
the doll in his belt she transferred it to her own possession, kissing it as she had kissed Korak.

Korak wanted to say something. He wanted to tell
her how he loved her, but the emotion of his love choked
him.

There came a sudden interruption. Akut had joined
them. Suddenly there came a low growl of warning from
the ape.

Korak looked quickly up from the glorious vision of
the sweet face so close to his. Now his other faculties
awoke. His ears, his nostrils were on the alert. Something
was coming!

Korak moved to Akut's side. Meriem was just behind
them. The three stood like carved statues gazing into the
leafy tangle of the jungle. The noise that had attracted
their attention increased, and presently a great ape broke
through the underbrush a few paces from where they
stood.

The beast halted at sight of them. He was followed
by others – both bulls and females with young – until
twoscore hairy monsters stood glaring at them. It was

the tribe of the dead king ape. Akut was the first to speak. He pointed to the body of the dead bull.

"Korak, mighty fighter, has killed your king," he grunted. "There is none greater in all the jungle than Korak, son of Tarzan. Now Korak is king. What bull is greater than Korak?"

It was a challenge to any bull who cared to question Korak's right to the kingship. The apes chattered and growled among themselves. At last a young bull came slowly forward rocking upon his short legs, bristling, growling, terrible. He was enormous, and in the full prime of his strength.

Korak advanced to meet the monster. He too was growling. In his mind a plan was revolving. To close with this powerful, untired brute after having just passed through a terrific battle with another of his kind would have been to tempt defeat. He must find an easier way to victory. Crouching, he prepared to meet the charge which he knew would soon come.

With clutching fingers and wide-opened jaws the great ape came down upon the waiting Korak with the speed of an express train. Korak did not move until the great arms swung to embrace him, then he swung a terrific right to the side of the beast's jaw and floored the ape.

It was a surprised anthropoid that attempted to scramble to its feet. Froth flecked its hideous lips. Red were the little eyes. Blood-curdling roars tumbled from the deep chest. But it did not reach its feet. Korak stood waiting, and the moment the hairy chin came up to its normal level another blow sent the ape over backward.

Again and again the beast struggled to rise. Each time the mighty Tarmangani stood waiting with ready fist and pile-driver blows to bowl him over. Weaker and weaker became the efforts of the bull. Blood smeared his face and breast. A red stream trickled from nose and mouth. The crowd that had cheered him on at first with savage yells, now jeered him – their cheers were for the Tarmangani.

"*Kagoda?*" inquired Korak, as he sent the bull down once more.

Again the stubborn bull tried to scramble to his feet. Again young Korak struck him a terrific blow. Again he put the question, *Kagoda* – have you had enough?

For a moment the bull lay motionless. Then from between battered lips came the single word: "*Kagoda!*"

"Then rise and go back among your people," said Korak. "I do not wish to be king among people who once drove me from them. Keep your own ways, and we will keep ours. When we meet we may be friends, but we shall not live together."

An old bull came slowly towards Korak.

"You have killed our king," he said. "You have defeated him who would have been king. You could have killed him had you wished. What shall we do for a king?"

Korak turned towards Akut.

"There is your king," he said. But Akut did not want to be separated from Korak, although he was anxious enough to remain with his own kind. He wanted Korak to remain, too. He said as much.

The youth was thinking of Meriem – of what would be best and safest for her. If Akut went away with the apes there would only be one to watch over and protect her. On the other hand, if they joined the tribe he would never feel safe leaving Meriem behind when he went out to hunt, for the passions of the ape-folk are not well controlled. A female might develop an insane hatred for the slender white girl and kill her during Korak's absence.

"We will live near you," he said, at last. "When you change your hunting-ground we will change ours, Meriem and I, and so remain near you. But we shall not dwell among you."

Akut raised objections to this plan. He did not wish to be separated from Korak. At first he refused to leave his human friend for the companionship of his own kind. But when he saw the tribe wandering off into the jungle again the call of blood would not be denied. With a farewell glance towards his beloved Korak he turned and followed the apes into the labyrinthine mazes of the wood.

Kovudoo was on the warpath. He and a party of warriors had come hunting far from their village, and one reason for the hunt was the hope that they might come across the great white ape who played tricks with their village.

Young Tarzan had several times silently entered the village, just as his father had entered other native villages long years before, sometimes to help himself to weapons, sometimes to food and clothing.

He had been discovered by accident and after that Kovudoo had hunted him, hoping to slay this white ape who stole things then ran laughing into the jungle. This day Kovudoo had found a trail where Korak and Meriem travelled earlier.

So it was that when Korak fought the great ape the sound of battle came to the ears of the natives and they arrived just in time to witness the astonishing events there in the glade.

Kovudoo saw the end of the battle and the victory of the white ape. He saw the other apes arrive, and witnessed the talk between them and Akut. And all the time his eyes were upon the slender white maiden in the midst of those hairy bodies. He could scarcely believe his eyes!

Finally the tribe of apes departed, and after a while Akut followed reluctantly, leaving the white ape with the white girl.

It was at this moment that one of Kovudoo's men came worming his way to the side of his chief.

"Look," he said, and pointed to something that dangled at the girl's side. "When my brother and I were slaves in the village of The Sheik my brother made that thing for The Sheik's daughter – she called it after my brother, whose name was Geeka. Just before we escape '

65

someone came and struck down The Sheik, stealing his daughter away. If this is she, The Sheik will pay you well for her return."

Korak's arm had again gone round the shoulders of Meriem. Love raced hot through his young veins. Again he drew her close to him and covered her willing lips with kisses. And then from behind broke a hideous bedlam of savage war-cries, and a score of shrieking warriors were upon them.

Korak turned to give battle. Meriem with her own light spear stood by his side. An avalanche of barbed missiles flew about them. One pierced Korak's shoulder, another his leg, and he went down.

Meriem was unscathed, for the natives had intentionally spared her. Now they rushed forward to finish Korak and make good the girl's capture. But as they came there charged from another point in the jungle the great Akut, and at his heels were the huge bulls of his new kingdom.

Snarling and roaring they rushed upon the warriors when they saw what had happened to Korak. Kovudoo, realizing the danger of coming to close quarters with these mighty ape-men, seized Meriem and called upon his warriors to retreat. For a time the apes followed them, and several of the natives were badly mauled and one killed before they succeeded in escaping.

Korak lay bleeding and unconscious when Akut reached his side. The great ape tore the heavy spears from his flesh, licked the wounds, and then carried his friend to the lofty shelter that Korak had constructed for Meriem. The brute could do no more than this. Nature must accomplish the rest unaided or Korak would die.

He did not die, however. For days he lay helpless with fever, while Akut and the apes hunted close by to protect him from snakes and beasts. Occasionally Akut brought him juicy fruits which helped to slake his thirst and allay his fever, and little by little his powerful constitution overcame the effects of the spear-thrusts. The wounds healed and his strength returned.

All during his rational moments he had suffered more from fears for Meriem than from the pain of his own wounds. For her he must live. For her he must regain his strength so that he might set out in search of her. What had the natives done to her? Did she still live, or had they sacrificed her to their lust for torture and human flesh? Korak trembled with terror at the hideous possibilities of the girl's fate.

The days dragged their weary lengths along, but at last he regained strength sufficiently to crawl from the shelter and make his way unaided to the ground. Now he lived on raw meat, for which he was entirely dependent on Akut's skill and generosity. With the meat diet his strength returned rapidly, and at last he felt that he was fit to undertake the journey to the village of the natives.

## The Fury of the Baboons

Two tall, bearded white men moved cautiously through the jungle from their camp beside a wide river. They were Carl Jenssen and Sven Malbihn, little altered in appearance since the day, years before, when they and their *safari* had been so badly frightened by Korak and Akut.

Every year they had come into the jungle to trade with the natives or to rob them, to hunt and trap, or to guide other white men in the land they knew so well. Always since their experience with The Sheik they had operated at a safe distance from his territory.

Now they were closer to his village than they had been for years. This year they had come to trap live specimens for a European zoological garden. Today they were approaching a trap which they had set in the hope of capturing a specimen of the large baboons that frequented the neighbourhood.

As they approached the trap they became aware from the noise that their efforts had been crowned with success. The barking and screaming of hundreds of baboons could only mean that one or more of their number had fallen a victim to the bait.

As they came within sight of the spot they found what they had expected. A large male was battering frantically against the steel wires of the cage that held him captive. Upon the outside several hundred other baboons were tearing and tugging at the wires, and all were roaring and barking at the top of their lungs. The prisoner was the king-baboon.

But what neither the Swedes nor the baboons saw was the half-naked figure of a youth hidden in the foliage of a nearby tree. He had come upon the scene at almost the same instant as Jenssen and Malbihn, and was watching the activities of the baboons with great interest.

Korak's relations with the baboons had never been very friendly, so now he was not greatly disturbed by the predicament of their king. Curiosity prompted him to tarry a moment, however, and in that moment his quick eyes caught the unfamiliar colour of the clothing of the two Swedes behind a bush. Instantly he was all alertness. Who were these interlopers? What was their business in the jungle of the Mangani?

Korak slunk noiselessly round them to a point where he could get their scent as well as a better view of them, and scarcely had he done so when he recognized them – they were the men who had fired on him years before.

His eyes blazed. He could feel the hairs upon his scalp stiffen at the roots. He watched them with the intentness of a panther about to spring upon its prey.

He saw them rise and, shouting, attempt to frighten away the baboons as they approached the cage. Then one of them raised his rifle and fired into the midst of the surprised and angry herd. For an instant Korak thought that the baboons were about to charge, but two more shots from the white men sent them scampering into the trees. Then the two Europeans advanced upon the cage.

Korak thought they were going to kill the king. He cared nothing for the king, but he cared less for the two white men. The king had never attempted to kill him – the white men had. The king was a denizen of his own beloved jungle – the white men were aliens. His loyalty, therefore, was to the baboon against the human. He could speak the language of the baboon – it was identical to that of the great apes. Across the clearing he saw the jabbering horde watching.

Raising his voice he shouted to them. "I am The Killer," he cried. "These men are my enemies and yours. I will help you free your king. Run out upon the strangers when you see me do so, and together we will drive them away and free your king."

And from the baboons came a great chorus: "We will do what you say, Korak."

Dropping from his tree, Korak ran towards the two Swedes, and instantly three hundred baboons followed his example. At sight of the strange apparition of the half-naked white warrior rushing upon them with uplifted spear Jenssen and Malbihn raised their rifles and fired at Korak. In the excitement both missed, and a moment later the baboons were upon them.

Now their only hope of safety lay in escape, and dodging here and there, fighting off the great beasts that leapt upon their backs, they ran into the jungle. Even then they would have died but for the coming of their men, whom they met a couple of hundred yards from the cage.

Once the white men had turned in flight Korak gave them no further attention, turning instead to the imprisoned baboon. A moment later the king baboon stepped forth to liberty.

He wasted no breath in thanks to Korak, nor did the young man expect thanks. He knew that none of the baboons would ever forget his service, though he did not care if they did. Now they were racing in the direction

69

of the battle that was being waged between their fellows and the followers of the two Swedes, and Korak turned and resumed his journey towards the village of Kovudoo.

On the way he came upon a herd of elephants standing in an open forest glade. Here the trees were too far apart to permit Korak to travel through the branches. The ape-man had to pass along the surface of the ground – a pygmy amongst giants.

A great bull raised his trunk to rattle a low warning as he sensed the coming of an intruder. His weak eyes roved hither and thither, but it was his keen scent and acute hearing which first located the ape-man. The herd moved restlessly, prepared for flight, for the old bull had caught the scent of man.

"Peace, Tantor," called Korak. "It is I, Korak, Tar-mangani."

The bull lowered his trunk and the herd quietened down. Korak passed within a foot of the great bull. A sinuous trunk undulated towards him, touching his brown hide in a half caress. Korak slapped the great shoulder affectionately as he went by.

For months he had been on good terms with Tantor and his people. Of all the jungle folk he loved the mighty pachyderm best – the most peaceful and at the same time the most terrible of them all. The gentle gazelle did not fear Tantor, yet Numa, lord of the jungle, gave him a wide berth. Among the younger bulls, the cows, and the calves Korak wound his way. Now and then another trunk would run out to touch him, and once a playful calf grasped his legs and upset him.

Darkness had come when Korak arrived at the village of Kovudoo. Keeping well in the shadows of the huts he began a systematic search of the village – ears, eyes, and nose constantly on the alert for the first sign of Meriem. His progress was slow, since not even the keen-eared curs of the savages must guess the presence of a stranger within the gates.

It was not until he reached the back of a hut at the

head of the wide village street that Korak caught the scent of Meriem. With nose close to the thatched wall Korak sniffed eagerly about the structure – tense as a hunting hound. Towards the front and the door he made his way when his nose assured him that Meriem lay within. But as he rounded the side and came within view of the entrance he saw a burly negro armed with a long spear squatting in the doorway of the girl's prison.

The fellow's back was towards him, his figure outlined against the glow of cooking fires farther down the street. He was alone. The nearest of his fellows were beside a fire sixty or seventy feet beyond. To enter the hut Korak had to silence the sentry or pass him unnoticed.

There was a good twelve inches of space between the broad back of the guard and the frame of the doorway. Could Korak pass behind the savage warrior without detection? The light that fell upon the glistening ebony of the sentry's black skin fell also upon the light brown of Korak's. Should one of the natives farther down the street chance to look in this direction they must surely note the tall, light-coloured, moving figure. Korak, however, reckoned upon their interest in their own gossip to hold their attention.

Flattened against the side of the hut, yet not arousing a single warning rustle from its dried thatching, Korak came closer and closer to the watcher. Now he was at his shoulder. Now he wormed his sinuous way behind him.

He could feel the heat of the naked body against his knees. He could hear the man breathe. He marvelled that the dull-witted creature had not long since been alarmed, but the fellow sat there as ignorant of his presence as if he did not exist.

Korak moved scarcely more than an inch at a time, then he would stand motionless for a moment. Thus was he worming his way behind the guard when the latter opened his cavernous mouth in a wide yawn, and stretched his arms above his head. Korak stood rigid as

71

stone. Another step and he would be within the hut. The warrior lowered his arms and relaxed. Behind him was the framework of the doorway. Often before it had supported his sleepy head, and now he leaned back to enjoy the forbidden pleasure of a cat nap.

But instead of the door frame his head and shoulders came in contact with the warm flesh of a pair of living legs. The exclamation of surprise that almost burst from his lips was throttled in his throat by steel-thewed fingers closing about his wind-pipe.

The warrior struggled to rise – to turn upon the creature that had seized him – to wriggle from its hold, but all to no purpose. As if held in a mighty vice of iron he could not move. He could not scream. Those awful fingers at his throat closed more and more tightly. Presently he relaxed once more.

Korak propped the body against the door frame. There it sat, lifelike in the gloom. Then the ape-man turned and glided into the Stygian darkness of the hut's interior.

"Meriem!" he whispered.

"Korak! My Korak!" came an answering cry, half stifled by a sob of joyful welcome.

The youth knelt and cut the bonds that held the girl's wrists and ankles. A moment later he lifted her to her feet, and grasping her by the hand led her towards the entrance.

Outside, the grim sentinel of death kept his grisly vigil. Sniffing at his feet whined a mangy native cur. At sight of the two emerging from the hut the beast gave an ugly snarl. An instant later, as it caught the scent of the strange white man, it raised a series of excited yelps. Instantly the warriors at the nearby fire were attracted. The turned their heads in the direction of the commotion. It was impossible that they could fail to see the white skins of the fugitives.

Korak slunk quickly into the shadows at the hut's side, drawing Meriem with him, but he was too late. The

72

natives had seen enough to arouse their suspicions, and a dozen of them were now running to investigate. The yapping cur was still at Korak's heels, leading the searchers unerringly in pursuit.

Other warriors had been alarmed by the running and shouting of their companions, and now the entire population of the village swarmed up the street to assist in the search. Their first discovery was the dead body of the sentry, and a moment later one of the bravest of them entered the hut and discovered the absence of the prisoner. This filled the natives with rage and, seeing no foe, they ran rapidly around the hut in the direction of the yapping cur. Here they found a single white warrior making away with their captive and believing they had him cornered they charged savagely upon him.

Korak, seeing that they were discovered, lifted Meriem to his shoulder and ran for the tree which would enable them to escape from the village. He was handicapped in his flight by the weight of the girl, whose legs could scarcely bear her weight. The tightly drawn bonds which had been about her ankles for so long had stopped the circulation and partially paralysed her limbs.

With the girl on his shoulder Korak could not both run and fight, so that before he had covered half the distance to the tree a score of native curs closed in upon the fleeing white man, snapping at his legs and at last succeeding in tripping him. As he went down the hyena-like brutes were upon him, and as he struggled to his feet the villagers closed in.

A couple of them seized the clawing, biting Meriem, and subdued her – a blow upon the head was sufficient. For the ape-man they found more drastic measures would be necessary. Weighted down as he was by dogs and warriors he still managed to struggle to his feet.

To right and left he swung crushing blows to the faces of his human antagonists – to the dogs he paid not the slightest attention. A knobstick aimed at him by an ebony Hercules he caught and wrested from his an-

73

tagonist, and then he rushed among the warriors with all the force and ferocity of a bull elephant gone mad.

Hither and thither he charged, striking down the few who had the temerity to stand against him. It was evident that unless a chance spear-thrust brought him down he would rout the entire village and regain his prize.

But old Kovudoo was not to be so easily robbed of the ransom which the girl represented. He saw that their weakness lay in the undisciplined attack, which had resulted in a series of individual combats with the white warrior. So now he called his tribesmen off, and forming them in a compact body about the girl bade them do nothing more than repel the assaults of the ape-man.

Again and again Korak rushed against this human barricade bristling with spear-points. Again and again he was repulsed. From head to foot he was red with his own blood, and at last came the bitter realization that alone he could do no more to rescue his Meriem.

Suddenly an idea flashed through his brain. He called aloud to the girl. She had regained consciousness now and replied.

"Korak goes," he shouted, "but he will return and take you from the Gomangani. Goodbye, my Meriem. Korak will come for you again."

"Goodbye!" cried the girl. "Meriem will look out for you."

Like a flash Korak wheeled, raced across the village, and with a single leap disappeared into the foliage of the great tree. A shower of spears followed him, but their only harvest was a taunting laugh flung back from the darkness of the jungle.

## In the Power of the Swedes

Meriem, again bound and under heavy guard in Kovudoo's own hut, saw the night pass and the new day come without bringing the return of Korak. She had no doubt he would come back and less still that he would easily free her from her captivity.

So now as she lay waiting for him she dreamed of him and of all that he meant to her. She compared him with The Sheik, her father, and at the thought of the stern, grizzled old Arab she shuddered. Even the savages had been less harsh to her than he.

She did not know that a runner had been dispatched to the distant village of The Sheik to barter with him for a ransom. She did not know, nor did Kovudoo, that the runner had never reached his destination – that he had fallen in with the *safari* of Jenssen and Malbihn and had unfolded his whole mission to the two Swedes.

When the runner left their camp to continue his journey he had scarcely passed from sight before there came the report of a rifle, and he rolled lifeless into the underbrush, with a bullet in his back.

A few moments later Malbihn strolled back into the encampment, where he went to some pains to let it be known that he had had a shot at a fine buck and missed.

The next day the Swedes set out for Kovudoo's village, bent on securing the white girl whom Kovudoo's runner had told them lay captive in the chief's village. It was the day following Korak's fight and flight from the village.

Their plans were well made. There was no mention of the girl – they chose to pretend that they were not aware that Kovudoo had a white prisoner. During the palaver which followed they retailed the gossip of the villages

75

through which they had passed, receiving in exchange such news as Kovudoo possessed.

Kovudoo also made no mention of his prisoner, and from his generous offers of guides and presents seemed anxious to encourage the speedy departure of his guests. It was Malbihn who, quite casually, near the close of their talk, mentioned the fact that The Sheik was dead. Kovudoo showed interest and surprise.

"You did not know it?" asked Malbihn. "That is strange. It was during the last moon. He fell from his horse when the beast stepped in a hole. The horse fell upon him. When his men came up The Sheik was quite dead."

Kovudoo scratched his head. He was disappointed. No Sheik meant no ransom for the white girl. Now she was worthless, unless he used her for a feast.

"I know where there is a white girl," he said unexpectedly. "If you wish to buy her she may be had cheap."

Malbihn shrugged. "We have troubles enough, Kovudoo," he said, "without burdening ourselves with an old she-hyena, and as for paying for one –" Malbihn snapped his fingers in derision.

"She is young," said Kovudoo, "and good-looking."

The Swedes laughed. "There are no good-looking white women in the jungle, Kovudoo," said Jenssen. "You should be ashamed to try to make fun of old friends."

Kovudoo sprang to his feet. "Come," he said. "I will show you that she is all I say."

Malbihn and Jenssen rose to follow him, and as they did so their eyes met, and Malbihn slowly drooped one of his lids in a sly wink. Together they followed Kovudoo towards his hut. In the dim interior they glimpsed the figure of a woman lying bound upon a sleeping-mat.

Malbihn took a single glance and turned away. "She must be a thousand years old, Kovudoo," he said, as he left the hut.

"She is young," cried the savage. "It is dark in here.

You cannot see. Wait, I will have her brought out into the sunlight," and he commanded the two warriors who watched the girl to cut the bonds from her ankles and lead her forth for inspection.

As Meriem was brought from the darkness of the hut's interior the two men turned with every appearance of disinterestedness to glance at her. It was with difficulty that Malbihn suppressed his astonishment. The girl's beauty fairly took his breath from him, but instantly he recovered his poise and turned to Kovudoo.

"Well?" he said to the old chief.

"Is she not both young and good-looking?" asked Kovudoo.

"She is not old," replied Malbihn. "Even so she will be a burden. We did not come from the north after wives – there are more than enough there for us."

Meriem stood looking straight at the white men. She expected nothing from them – they were to her as much enemies as the black men. She hated and feared them all. Malbihn spoke to her in Arabic.

"We are friends," he said. "Would you like us to take you away from here?"

Slowly and dimly, as though from a great distance, recollection of the once familiar tongue returned to her.

"I should like to go free," she said, "and go back to Korak."

"You would like to go with us?" persisted Malbihn.

"No," said Meriem.

Malbihn turned to Kovudoo. "She does not wish to go with us," he said.

"You are men," returned the black. "Can you not take her by force?"

"It would only add to our troubles," replied the Swede. "No, Kovudoo, we do not want her. But if you wish to be rid of her, we will take her away because of our friendship for you."

Now Kovudoo knew he had made a sale. They wanted her. So he began to bargain, and in the end Meriem pas-

sed from the possession of the black chieftain into that of
the two Swedes in consideration of six yards of American
cloth, three empty brass cartridge shells, and a shiny,
new jack-knife from New Jersey. And all except Meriem
were more than pleased with the bargain.

Kovudoo made only one condition, and that was that
the Europeans were to leave his village and take the girl
with them as early the next morning as they could get
started. After the sale was concluded he explained his
reasons for this demand. He told them of the strenuous
attempt of the girl's savage mate to rescue her, and suggested that the sooner they got her out of the country
the more likely they were to retain possession of her.

Meriem was again bound and placed under guard, but
this time in the tent of the Swedes. Malbihn talked to her,
trying to persuade her to accompany them willingly. He
told her they would return her to her own village, but
when he discovered that she would rather die than go
back to the old Sheik he then promised they would not
take her there.

As he talked with the girl the Swede feasted his eyes
upon the beautiful lines of her face and figure. She had
grown tall and straight since he had first seen her in The
Sheik's village long ago.

For years she had represented to him a certain fabu-
lous reward. Now, as she stood before him pulsing with
life and loveliness, she suggested other possibilities.

He came closer to her and laid his hand upon her.
The girl shrank from him. He seized her, and she struck
him heavily on the mouth as he sought to kiss her. Then
Jenssen entered the tent.

"Malbihn!" he almost shouted. "You fool!"

Sven Malbihn released his hold upon the girl and
turned towards his companion. His face was red with
mortification.

"What the devil are you trying to do?" growled Jenssen. "Would you throw away every chance for the reward? If we maltreat her we not only couldn't collect a

sou, but they'd send us to prison for our pains. I thought you had more sense, Malbihn."

"I'm not a wooden man," growled Malbihn.

"You'd better be," rejoined Jenssen – "at least until we have delivered her over in safety and collected the reward."

Malbihn gave his friend an ugly look, shrugged his shoulders, and left the tent. Jenssen turned to Meriem.

"If he bothers you again, call me," he said. "I shall always be near."

The girl had not understood the conversation, for it had been in Swedish, but what Jenssen had just said to her in Arabic she understood, and from it grasped an excellent idea of what had passed between the two. The expressions upon their faces, their gestures, and Jenssen's final tapping of his revolver before Malbihn left the tent had all been eloquent.

Now, towards Jenssen she looked for friendship, and with the innocence of youth she threw herself upon his mercy, begging him to set her free, that she might return to Korak and her jungle life. She was doomed to another disappointment however for the man only laughed at her roughly and told her that if she tried to escape she would be punished.

All that night she lay listening for a signal from Korak. All about the jungle life moved through the darkness. To her sensitive ears came sounds that the others in the camp could not hear – sounds that she interpreted as we might interpret the speech of a friend, but not once came a single note that told of the presence of Korak. But she knew that he would come. Nothing short of death itself could prevent her Korak from returning for her. What delayed him, then?

When morning came again and the night had brought no Korak, Meriem's faith and loyalty were still unshaken though misgivings began to assail her as to the safety of her friend. It seemed unbelievable that serious mishap could have overtaken her wonderful Korak, who daily passed unscathed through all the terrors of the jungle.

Yet morning came, the morning meal was eaten, the camp broken, and the disreputable *safari* of the Swedes was on the move northward with still no sign of the rescue the girl momentarily expected.

All that day they marched, and the next and the next, nor did Korak even so much as show himself to the patient girl moving silently and stately beside her hard captors.

Malbihn remained scowling and angry. He replied to Jenssen's friendly advances in curt monosyllables. To Meriem he did not speak, but on several occasions she discovered him glaring at her from beneath half-closed lids – greedily. The look sent a shudder through her. She hugged Geeka closer to her breast, and doubly regretted the knife they had taken from her when she was captured by Kovudoo.

It was on the fourth day that Meriem began to give up hope. Something had happened to Korak. He would never come now, and these men would take her far away.

Towards evening, Meriem was placed in her tent as usual. One end of an ancient slave chain was fastened to an iron collar padlocked around her neck. The other end was bolted to a long iron stake driven deep into the ground. Her hands and feet were not fettered, so that she could move around the tent.

As she sat there, wretched and despairing, she thought of Korak and the wonderful life she had lived with him in the jungle – the happiest period of her existence, she told herself. Then inevitably her thoughts came back to Jenssen and Malbihn, and she wondered what they were going to do with her.

While she was sitting there, suddenly the tent flap was drawn quickly open. Malbihn came in. Startled, poor Meriem rose to her feet. Malbihn stood there, his red-rimmed eyes glistening unpleasantly. Meriem's heart bounded. She was afraid.

80

He grinned and came towards her, somehow stealthy in his movements. Wide-eyed with terror, Meriem retreated as far as the chain would permit. All at once Malbihn sprang, too quickly for her to cry out. Meriem found herself gripped around the body by one arm and hand, while the other was clapped across her mouth to quieten her.

For one instant, Meriem was helpless in his grip. The next moment Malbihn found he had caught a tiger.

Meriem bit and kicked and wriggled. Her tough sinewy body, built up by her days in the trees with Korak, startled him by its strength. Malbihn shouted with pain as her teeth bit hard and deep into his hand. He dragged it away. Meriem's mouth was free. She began to scream for help – though who would help her in that camp?

Malbihn became furious at her resistance, and tried again to hold her and gag her mouth. But she was a bundle of fury in his arms, holding him off for the second, though in the end his superior man's strength would win.

Again, though, the tent flap was flung open. Looking over Malbihn's shoulder, Meriem saw the furious face of Jenssen. Jenssen came leaping forward, shouting, "You drunken fool! That girl's worth a fortune to us. Do you want to wreck it all?"

His hand came whipping down, cracking Malbihn hard across the face. Blood spurted. Meriem felt the grip relax and she pulled herself away from the staggering Malbihn. The tent was too small with three people inside it. Outside Meriem heard the voices of the bearers, excited by the sounds of quarrelling between white men.

Jenssen said, "You keep your hands off her –"

Meriem screamed. Malbihn was rising off the ground. His face was contorted with rage. He was drawing a gun. Jenssen saw it and was startled. He stepped back in alarm. "Put that away –" he began.

Malbihn fired from one knee. Fired deliberately. Meriem saw Jenssen's body jerk as the first bullet hit him. A second bullet caught him and spun him round. A

81

third bullet hit him in the head as he was falling. He was dead before he hit the ground.

Shocked, Meriem could only stare at the body of the murdered man. Outside the bearers were shouting shrilly, half-pleased, half-afraid. Malbihn seemed in a bit of a daze, too. Then his head came round so that he looked at the shrinking Meriem. His eyes narrowed.

"May as well finish it," she heard him say, then he lurched forward and grabbed her, the gun still in his hand. The fight had gone out of her with the brutal murder. She could only look with horror into those cold merciless eyes.

Late that afternoon a white hunter had seen smoke rising from a distant camp. It puzzled him to know who could be in that remote part of Africa, and anyway one hunter always came to share another hunter's fire, so he ordered his boys – a smiling, cheerful lot – to head that way.

They were a few hundred yards from the camp and could see the protective *boma* erected to keep out the jungle predators, when first they heard a girl scream, then the sound of shots.

The big white man was startled and hurried forward. He saw frightened bearers clustered together, eyes staring towards a tent. Inside something moved. The white man came to it and pulled back the flap.

He saw a dead man on the ground, new blood bright on the face. He saw a lithe and sinewy girl, very brown, slave-collared to an iron stake, and a big, bearded, sweat-stained blond man holding her in a painful grasp. He also saw in that quick glance a gun in the man's right hand.

The big man moved so smoothly, so swiftly, yet somehow everything he did spoke of power. Malbihn found hands grasping him that made him helpless. The gun was torn from his grasp and tossed away. Then he was pulled away from the girl and sent spinning, to crash down to the ground again. And it was so effortlessly done that if he had had sense he would have stayed there.

Instead he had to try to get revenge on the big white man who had assaulted him. He came lurching up, mouthing curses. The big man hit him – only once. Malbihn went sick, sagging to his knees, then sprawling on to his face.

Meriem stood there, trembling. Grey eyes swung to her, kindly, compassionately. "Are you all right?" He spoke in English.

The girl did not understand. In Arabic she began to say, "Get me away! Oh, help me!" then burst into tears.

The big man reached out to console her, but Meriem instantly drew back in fear. The man shook his head. "Have no fear," he said in Arabic. "I shall not hurt you."

Meriem looked at him, big and kindly, mighty and strong, and her fear left her. This man would not harm a girl, she knew. He asked her what had happened, and Meriem told him in Arabic.

"They took me away – I don't know where they were taking me. He killed his friend, quarrelling over me. Do help me!"

Once more he soothed her. Malbihn was staggering dazedly to his feet. The big man spoke to him, and his voice rasped like cold steel on ice.

"I do not approve of slavery. I am taking this girl away from you. If there was any law and justice in the jungle I would hand you over to stand trial for murder. But there is none and I cannot take your life myself. Now, get out of here. Pack up and leave this country. For if ever I set eyes on you again it might go hard for you."

Malbihn swayed, listening, then staggered out of the tent, glad to have escaped with his life from the presence of that huge and formidable white man. They heard him shouting to his porters to strike camp, they were moving on until darkness.

"Now," the man said, turning towards Meriem, "who has the key to this thing about your neck?"

The girl pointed to Jenssen's body.

The stranger searched the clothing on the corpse until he came upon the key. A moment more Meriem was free.

"Will you let me go back to my Korak?" she asked.

"I will see you are returned to your people," he replied. "Who are they, and where is their village?"

He had been eyeing her strange, barbaric garments wonderingly. From her speech she was evidently an Arab girl.

"Who are your people? Who is Korak?" he asked again.

"Korak! Why, Korak is an ape. I have no other people."

A questioning expression entered the stranger's eyes. He looked at the girl closely.

"So Korak is an ape?" he said. "And what are you?"

"I am Meriem. I also am an ape."

"M-m," was the stranger's only comment. And then – "How long have you been an ape?" asked the man.

"Since I was a little girl, many, many moons ago, when Korak came and took me from my father who was beating me. Since then I have lived in the trees with Korak and A'ht." That was her way of saying Akut.

"Where in the jungle lives Korak?" asked the stranger.

Meriem pointed with a sweep of her hand that took in, generously, half the continent of Africa.

"Could you find your way back to him?"

"I do not know," she replied, "but he will find his way to me."

"Then I have a plan," said the stranger. "I live but a few marches from here. I shall take you home where my wife will care for you until we find Korak or Korak finds us. If he could find you here he can find you at my village. Is that not so?"

84

The stranger remained until Malbihn and his *safari* disappeared into the jungle towards the north. Meriem, trustful now, stood at his side, Geeka clutched in one slim, brown hand. They talked together, the man wondering at the faltering Arabic of the girl. Then, still holding Meriem's hand, the man called to his boys and they set off through the jungle.

On the fifth day they came suddenly upon a great plain, and from the edge of the forest the girl saw in the distance fenced fields and many buildings. She drew back in astonishment.

"Where are we?" she asked, pointing.

"That is my home," smiled the man. "I have brought you here to wait and rest with my wife until my men can find your ape, or he finds you. It is better thus, little one. You will be safer with us, and you will be happier."

"I am afraid, Bwana," said the girl. "In thy *douar* they will beat me as did The Sheik, my father. Let me go back into the jungle. There Korak will find me. He would not think to look for me in the *douar* of a white man."

"No one will beat you, child," replied the man. "I have not done so, have I? Here no one is beaten. My wife will be very good to you, and at last Korak will come, for I shall send men to search for him."

The girl shook her head. "They could not bring him, for he would kill them, as all men have tried to kill him. I am afraid. Let me go, Bwana."

"You do not know the way to your own country. You would be lost. The leopards or the lions would get you the first night."

Meriem laughed. "The jungle," she said, "is my father and my mother. It has been kinder to me than men. No, I do not fear the jungle. I love it. But you have been good to me. I will do as you wish, and remain here for a while to wait the coming of my Korak."

"Good!" said the man, and he led the way towards

85

the flower-covered bungalow behind which lay the barns and outhouses of a well-ordered African farm.

Meriem walked on towards the bungalow, at the porch of which a woman dressed in white waved a welcome to her returning lord. There was more fear in the girl's eyes now than there had been in the presence of strange men or savage beasts. She hesitated, turning an appealing glance towards the man.

"That is my wife," he said. "She will be glad to welcome you."

The woman came down the path to meet them. The man kissed her, and turning towards Meriem introduced them, speaking in the Arab tongue the girl understood.

"This is Meriem, my dear," he said, and he told the story of the jungle waif so far as he knew it.

Meriem saw that the woman was beautiful. She saw that sweetness and goodness were stamped indelibly upon her countenance. She no longer feared her, and when the woman came and put her arms about her and kissed her and called her "poor little darling," something snapped in Meriem's heart.

She buried her face on the bosom of this new friend in whose voice was the mother-tone that Meriem had not heard for so many years that she had forgotten its very existence. She buried her face on the kindly bosom and wept as she had not wept before in all her life – tears of relief and joy that she could not fathom.

And so came Meriem, the savage little Mangani, out of her beloved jungle into the midst of a home of culture and refinement. Already "Bwana" and "My Dear," as she first heard them called, were as father and mother to her. Once her savage fears were allayed, she went to the opposite extreme of trustfulness and love. Now she was willing to wait until they found Korak, or Korak found her.

And out in the jungle, far away, Korak, covered with wounds, stiff with clotted blood, burning with rage and sorrow, swung back upon the trail of the great baboons. He had not found them where he had last seen them, nor in any of their usual haunts, so he sought them along the well-marked spoor they had left behind them, and at last he overtook them.

When first he came upon them they were moving slowly but steadily southward in one of those periodic migrations the reasons for which the baboon himself is best able to explain. At sight of the white warrior who came upon them from downwind the herd halted.

There was much growling and muttering, much stiff-legged circling on the part of the bulls. The mothers, in nervous, high-pitched tones, called their young to their sides, and with them moved to safety behind their lords and masters.

Korak called aloud to the king, who at the familiar voice advanced slowly, warily, and still stiff-legged. He needed the confirmatory evidence of his nose before venturing to rely upon his ears and eyes. Korak stood perfectly still.

The king baboon approached Korak. He walked around him in an ever-decreasing circle – growling, grunting, sniffing. Korak spoke to him.

"I am Korak," he said. "I opened the cage that held you. I saved you from the Tarmangani. I am Korak, The Killer. I am your friend."

"Huh!" grunted the king. "Yes, you are Korak. My ears told me you were Korak. My eyes told me you were Korak. Now my nose tells me you are Korak. My nose is never wrong. I am your friend. Come, we shall hunt together."

87

"Korak cannot hunt now," replied the ape-man. "The Gomangani have stolen Meriem. They have tied her in their village. They will not let her go. Korak, alone, was unable to set her free. Korak set you free. Now will you bring your people and set Korak's Meriem free?"

"The Gomangani have many sharp sticks which they throw. They pierce the bodies of my people. They kill us. The Gomangani are bad people. They will kill us all if we enter their village."

"The Tarmangani have sticks that make a loud noise and kill at a great distance," replied Korak. "They had these when Korak set you free from their trap. If Korak had run away from them you would now be a prisoner among the Tarmangani."

The baboon scratched his head. In a rough circle about him and the ape-man squatted the bulls of his herd. They blinked their eyes, shouldered one another about for more advantageous positions, scratched in the rotting vegetation upon the chance of unearthing a toothsome worm, or sat listlessly eyeing their king and the strange Mangani.

The King looked at some of the older of his subjects, as though inviting suggestion.

"We are too few," grunted one.

"There are the baboons of the hill country," suggested another. "They are as many as the leaves of the forest. They, too, hate the Gomangani. They love to fight. They are very savage. Let us ask them to accompany us. Then can we kill all the Gomangani in the jungle."

He rose and growled horribly, bristling his stiff hair.

Korak could not persuade them. They would help him gladly, but they must do it in their own way, and that meant enlisting the services of their kinsmen and allies of the hill country. So Korak was forced to give in. All he could do for the present was to urge them to hurry, and at his suggestion the king baboon with a dozen of his mightiest bulls agreed to go to the hill country with Korak, leaving the rest of the herd behind.

Once enlisted in the adventure the baboons became quite enthusiastic about it. The delegation set off immediately. They travelled swiftly, but the ape-man found no difficulty in keeping up with them. They made a tremendous racket as they passed through the trees in order to suggest to enemies that a great herd was approaching, for when baboons travel in large numbers there is no jungle creature who cares to molest them.

For two days the party raced through the savage country, passing out of the dense jungle into an open plain, and across this to timbered mountain slopes.

Once in the forest the baboons advanced more slowly. Constantly they gave tongue to a plaintive note of calling. At last, faintly from the distance ahead came an answer.

The baboons continued to travel in the direction of the voices. Thus, calling and listening they came closer to their kinsmen, who were coming in great numbers. When at last the baboons of the hill country came into view the ape-man was staggered at their numbers.

What appeared a solid wall of huge baboons rose from the ground. Slowly they approached, voicing their weird, plaintive call, and behind them, as far as Korak's eyes could see, rose solid walls of their fellows treading close upon their heels. There were thousands of them.

The two kings approached one another, as was their custom, with much sniffing and bristling. They satisfied themselves of each other's identity. Then each scratched the other's back. After a moment they spoke together.

Korak's friend explained the nature of their visit, and for the first time Korak showed himself. The excitement among the hill baboons was intense. For a moment Korak feared he would be torn to pieces.

The two kings, however, managed to quieten the multitude, and Korak was permitted to approach. Slowly the hill baboons came closer. They sniffed at him from every angle. When he spoke in their own tongue they were filled with wonder and delight. They talked to him and listened while he spoke. He told them of Meriem, and of their life in the jungle where they were the friends of all the ape folk from little Manu to Mangani, the great ape.

"The Gomangani, who are keeping Meriem from me, are no friends of yours," he said. "They kill you. The baboons of the low country are too few to go against them. They tell me that you are very many and very brave – that your numbers are as the numbers of the grasses upon the plains or the leaves within the forest, and that even Tantor, the elephant, fears you. They tell me you would be happy to accompany us to the village of the Gomangani and punish these bad people while I, Korak, The Killer, carry away my Meriem."

The king ape puffed out his chest and strutted about very stiff-legged indeed. So also did many of the other great bulls of his nation. They were pleased and flattered by the words of the strange Tarmangani.

"Yes," said one, "we of the hill country are mighty fighters. Tantor fears us. Numa fears us. Sheeta fears us. The Gomangani of the hill country are glad to pass us by in peace. I, for one, will come with you to the village of the Gomangani of the low places. Alone can I kill all the Gomangani of the low country," and he swelled his chest and strutted proudly back and forth.

"I am Goob," cried another. "My fighting fangs are long. Goob will go to the low country with you and kill so many of the Gomangani that there will be none left to count the dead," and then he too strutted and pranced before the admiring eyes of the shes and the young.

Korak looked at the king questioningly.

"Your bulls are very brave," he said, "but braver than any is the king."

Thus addressed, the shaggy bull, still in his prime growled ferociously. The forest echoed to his lusty challenges. The little baboons clutched fearfully at their mother's hairy necks. The bulls, electrified, leaped high in the air and took up the roaring challenge of their king. The din was terrific.

Korak came close to the king and shouted in his ear,

90

"Come!" Then he started off through the forest. The king, still roaring wheeled and followed him. In their wake came the handful of low-country baboons and the thousands of the hill clan – savage, wiry, doglike creatures athirst for blood.

And so they came, upon the second day, to the village of Kovudoo. It was mid-afternoon. The village was sunk in the quiet of the great equatorial sun-heat. The mighty herd travelled noiselessly now.

Korak and the two kings were in the lead. Close beside the village they halted until the stragglers closed up. Now utter silence reigned. Korak, creeping stealthily, entered the tree that overhung the palisade. He glanced behind him. The pack were close upon his heels. The time had come.

He had warned them continuously during the long march that no harm must befall the white she who lay a prisoner within the village. All others were their legitimate prey. Then, raising his face towards the sky, he gave voice to a single cry. It was the signal.

In response, three thousand hairy bulls leaped screaming and barking into the village of the terrified natives. Warriors poured from every hut. Mothers gathered their babes in their arms and fled towards the gates as they saw the horde pouring into the village street. Kovudoo marshalled his fighting men about him, and leaping and yelling to rouse their courage, offered a bristling, spear-tipped front to the charging horde.

Korak, as he had led the march, led the charge. The natives were struck with horror and dismay at sight of this white-skinned youth at the head of a pack of hideous baboons. For an instant they held their ground, hurling their spears at the advancing multitude, but before they could fit arrows to their bows they wavered, gave, and turned in terrified rout.

At the village gates, through which the natives poured in panic, Korak left them to the tender mercies of his allies and turned eagerly towards the hut in which

91

Meriem had been a prisoner. It was empty. One after another the filthy interiors revealed the same disheartening fact – Meriem was in none of them. She had not been taken by the blacks in their flight from the village, Korak knew, for he had watched carefully for a glimpse of her among the fugitives.

To the mind of the ape-man, knowing as he did the habits of the savages, there was only one explanation – Meriem had been killed and eaten. With the conviction that Meriem was dead there surged through Korak's brain a wave of blood-red rage against those he believed to be her murderer.

In the distance he could hear the snarling of the baboons mixed with the screams of their victims, and towards this he made his way.

Among these broke Korak from the branches of a tree above them – swift, relentless, terrible, he hurled himself upon the savage warriors of Kovudoo. Blind fury possessed him. Like a wounded lioness he was here, there, everywhere, striking terrible blows. Those who could fled, until at last there were none to face Korak and the baboons. Panting and bloody, Korak paused. The baboons gathered round him.

In the distance Kovudoo was gathering his scattered tribesmen, and taking account of injuries and losses. His people were panic-stricken. Nothing could induce them to remain longer in this country. They would not even return to the village for their belongings. Instead, they insisted upon continuing their flight.

And thus it was that Korak drove from their homes the only people who might have aided him in his search for Meriem.

# Meriem and Numa

To Meriem, in her new home, the days passed quickly. At first she was all anxiety to be off into the jungle searching for her Korak. Bwana, as she insisted upon calling her benefactor, dissuaded her by dispatching a headman with a party of natives to Kovudoo's village, with instructions to learn from the old savage how he came into possession of the white girl.

Bwana also charged his head-man with the duty of questioning Kovudoo about the strange character whom the girl called Korak, and of searching for the ape-man if he existed.

Bwana was convinced at first that Korak was a creature of the girl's disordered imagination. He believed that the terrors and hardships she had undergone during captivity had unbalanced her mind. As the days passed, however, and he became better acquainted with her he was forced to admit that her strange tale puzzled him, for there was no other evidence that Meriem was not in full possession of her normal faculties.

A month passed before the head-man returned – a month that had transformed the savage, half-naked little Tarmangani into a daintily frocked girl of at least outward civilization. Meriem had progressed rapidly with the intricacies of the English language, for Bwana and My Dear persistently refused to speak Arabic.

The report of the head-man plunged Meriem into despondency, for he had found the village of Kovudoo deserted. For some time he had camped near the village, spending the days in a systematic search for traces of Meriem's Korak, but in this quest he too had failed. He had seen neither apes nor ape-man.

Meriem at first insisted upon setting out herself in

search of Korak, but Bwana prevailed upon her to wait. He would go himself, he assured her, as soon as he could find the time, and at last Meriem consented to abide by his wishes. It was months, though, before she ceased to mourn almost hourly for Korak.

She was sixteen now, though she might easily have passed for nineteen, and she was good to look upon, with her black hair and tanned skin. She spoke English fluently now, and read and wrote it as well. One day My Dear spoke jokingly to her in French, and to her surprise Meriem replied in the same tongue – slowly, it is true, and haltingly, but none the less in excellent French.

"You doubtless heard French spoken at times in your father's *douar*," suggested My Dear, as the most reasonable explanation.

Meriem shook her head.

"It may be," she said, "but I do not recall ever having seen a Frenchman in my father's company. He hated them. I cannot understand it."

"Neither can I," agreed My Dear.

It was about this time that a runner brought a letter that, when she learned the contents, filled Meriem with excitement. Visitors were coming! A number of English ladies and gentlemen had accepted My Dear's invitation to spend a month of hunting and exploring with them. Meriem was all expectancy. What would these strangers be like? Would they be as nice to her as Bwana and My Dear, or would they be like the other white folk she had known – cruel and relentless?

At last the visitors arrived. There were three men and two women – the wives of the two older men. The youngest member of the party was Morison Baynes, a young man of considerable wealth who, having exhausted all the possibilities for pleasure offered by the capitals of Europe, had gladly seized upon this opportunity to turn to another continent for excitement and adventure.

Baynes was a good-looking young man, very courteous and gallant to the ladies. He was also a spoilt young man,

94

getting what he wanted, with little thought to others. Spoilt and somewhat selfish, but beneath it all there was something rather good about his character which on occasions showed. Perhaps Baynes' main trouble was thoughtlessness – he had never had to want and suffer and did not understand this in the lives of others.

Meriem, at first, was shy and reserved in the presence of the strangers. Her benefactors did not mention her strange past, and she passed as their ward. The guests found her sweet and unassuming, laughing, vivacious, and a never-exhausted storehouse of quaint and interesting jungle lore.

She had ridden much during her year with Bwana and My Dear. She knew each clump of concealing reeds along the river that the buffalo loved best. She knew a dozen places where lions laired, and every drinking-hole in the drier country twenty-five miles back from the river. With unerring precision she could track the largest or the smallest beast to his hiding-place. But the thing that baffled them all was her instant consciousness of the presence of carnivora that others could neither see nor hear.

Baynes found Meriem a most beautiful and charming companion. He was delighted with her from the first. They were together a great deal, as they were the only unmarried couple in the little company. Meriem, entirely unaccustomed to men like Baynes, was fascinated by him.

With the companionship of the young Englishman the image of Korak became less real. Korak was now only a memory though to that memory she was still loyal.

Meriem had never accompanied the men on a hunt since the arrival of the guests. She had never cared particularly for the sport of killing. Tracking she enjoyed, but the mere killing for the sake of killing she could not find pleasure in.

When Bwana went forth to shoot for meat she had always been his enthusiastic companion, but with the coming of the London guests the hunting deteriorated into mere killing. Slaughter the host would not permit, yet the purpose of the hunts was for heads and skins and not for food.

So Meriem remained behind, and spent her days either with My Dear upon the shaded veranda, or riding her favourite pony to the forest edge. Here she would leave him untethered, while she took to the trees in a brief return to the wild, free existence of her earlier life.

At such time would come visions of Korak and, tired at last of swinging through the trees, she would stretch herself comfortably upon a branch and dream. And presently, as today, she found the features of Korak slowly dissolve and merge into those of another, and the figure of a tanned, half-naked Tarmangani became a khaki-clothed Englishman astride a hunting pony.

And while she dreamed, there came to her ears from a distance, faintly, the terrified bleating of a kid. Meriem was instantly alert. To her the sound told of the terror of the goat when a carnivore is near and escape impossible.

It had been both a pleasure and a sport of Korak's to rob Numa of his prey whenever possible, and Meriem too had often snatched some dainty morsel from the very jaws of the king of the beasts. Now, at the sound of the kid's bleat, all the well-remembered thrills returned. Instantly she was determined to play again the game of hide-and-seek with death.

Quickly she loosened her riding-skirt and tossed it aside. Her boots and stockings followed the skirt. At her hip hung a hunting-knife. Her rifle was still in its boot at her pony's withers.

The kid was still bleating as Meriem started rapidly in its direction. She wondered why the sounds continued from the same point. Why did the kid not run away? And then she came in sight of the little animal and knew. The kid was tethered to a stake beside the water-hole.

96

Meriem paused and scanned the clearing with quick penetrating eyes. Where was the hunter? Ah! Now she saw him. He was lying in a clump of brush a few yards to her right. The kid was downwind from him and getting the full effect of his terrifying scent.

To circle to the opposite side of the clearing, where the trees approached closer to the kid, to leap quickly to the little animal's side and cut the tether that held him, would be the work of a moment. But in that moment Numa might charge, and then there would not be time to regain the safety of the trees.

Again the kid struggled to be free. Again his piteous wail touched the tender heart-strings of the girl. Tossing discretion aside, she began to circle the clearing.

At last she reached the opposite trees. An instant later she paused to look towards the great lion, and at the same moment she saw the huge beast rise slowly to his full height.

Meriem loosened her knife and leapt to the ground. A quick run brought her to the side of the kid. Numa saw her. He lashed his tail against his tawny sides and roared terribly but remained where he stood – surprised by the strange apparition that had sprung so unexpectedly from the jungle.

Other eyes were upon Meriem too. A white man, hiding in a thorn *boma*, half rose as the young girl leapt into the clearing and dashed towards the kid. He saw Numa hesitate. He raised his rifle and covered the beast's breast. The girl reached the kid's side. Her knife flashed, and the little prisoner was free. With a parting bleat it dashed off into the jungle. Then the girl turned towards the safety of the tree.

As she turned, the white man caught sight of the girl's face. He gave a little gasp of surprise, but now the lion demanded all his attention – the baffled, angry beast was charging. The man could have fired and stopped the charge at once, but for some reason he hesitated. Could

97

it be that he did not want to save her? Or did he prefer to remain unseen by her?

Like an eagle the man watched the race for life that the girl was making. Not once did the rifle sights fail to cover the broad breast of the tawny lion.

Once, at the very last moment, when escape seemed impossible, the hunter's finger tightened slightly on the trigger, but at that moment the girl leapt for an overhanging branch and seized it. The lion leapt too, but the nimble Meriem had swung herself beyond his reach without a second to spare.

The man breathed a sigh of relief as he lowered his rifle. He saw the girl laugh at the roaring man-eater beneath her and then speed away into the forest. For an hour the lion remained about the water-hole, then at last Numa, still roaring angrily, strode majestically into the jungle.

The hunter crawled from his *boma*, and half an hour later entered a little camp snugly hidden in the forest. He was a great bearded man, a huge, yellow-bearded giant, when he entered his tent. Half an hour later he emerged smooth shaven.

His bearers looked at him in astonishment.

"Would you know me?" he asked.

"The hyena that bore you would not know you, Bwana," replied one.

The man aimed a heavy fist at the black's face, but long experience in dodging similar blows saved the insolent native.

## Baynes Shows Cunning

Meriem returned slowly towards the tree in which she had left her clothes. She was singing blithely, but her song came to a sudden stop when she came within sight of the tree, for there, pulling and hauling upon her belongings, were a number of baboons. When they saw

98

her they showed no signs of terror. Instead they bared their fangs and growled at her. What was there to fear in a single she-Tarmangani? Nothing, absolutely nothing.

In the open plain beyond the forest the hunters were returning from the day's sport. They were widely separated, hoping to raise a wandering lion on the homeward journey across the plain. Baynes rode closest to the forest. As his eyes wandered across the undulating ground, he noticed something at the edge of the jungle. As he came closer he saw it was a horse. He approached and, as he did so, his eyes glinted with pleasure for he recognized the pony as the special favourite of Meriem.

He galloped to the animal's side. Meriem must be within the wood. He dismounted and left his horse beside Meriem's. On foot he entered the jungle, hoping to surprise her by coming suddenly upon her.

He had only gone a short distance into the wood when he heard a great jabbering in a nearby tree. Coming closer he saw a band of baboons snarling over something. Looking intently, he saw that one of them held a woman's riding-skirt while others had boots and stockings. His heart almost ceased to beat. The baboons had killed Meriem and stripped this clothing from her body!

He was about to call for help when he saw her in a tree close to the baboons. They were snarling and jabbering at her. To his amazement, he saw the girl swing, ape-like, into the tree below the huge beasts. He almost dropped his rifle in surprise as the strange jabbering, identical to that of the apes, broke from Meriem's lips.

The baboons stopped their snarling and listened. For several minutes the girl carried on a conversation with the baboons, and then her clothing was handed over to her.

The baboons crowded eagerly about her as she put them on. They chattered to her and she chattered back. Baynes sat down at the foot of a tree and mopped his perspiring brow. Then he rose and made his way back to his mount.

When Meriem emerged from the forest a few minutes later she found him there, and he gazed at her with wide eyes in which were both wonder and a sort of terror.

"I saw your horse," he explained, "and thought I would wait and ride home with you. You do not mind?"

"Of course not," she replied. "It will be lovely."

As they made their way across the plain, Baynes secretly watched the girl's profile and wondered if his eyes deceived him or if he really had seen this lovely creature talking fluently with grotesque baboons. The thing was bewildering, impossible. Yet he had seen it with his own eyes.

Baynes mopped his brow. Meriem noticed the action and said, innocently, "You are hot. But why? The sun is setting."

Baynes hesitated, then came out with it. "I saw you," he blurted out. "Up there, talking to the baboons."

"But they are my friends," said Meriem unemotionally.

"Friends?" He was shocked. "Those – those terrifying beasts."

"Great friends," said Meriem and suddenly she was in the mood to tease him. "Not long ago I lived among them – among the animals of the jungle. That is where I learned to speak their language. I lived almost naked, my home in the trees, with A'ht and Korak as my two greatest friends."

"A'ht and Korak!" repeated Baynes, and his head was in a daze. "Who," he asked, trying to make sense of the conversation, "are A'ht and Korak?"

"Korak," said Meriem, her eyes shining, "is the most wonderful ape on earth – a white ape. A'ht is his greatest friend."

Baynes could only shake his head, not understanding at all. Meriem was too bewildering a companion for an ordinary man to keep pace with her conversation.

But Meriem was also a gloriously beautiful girl, and Baynes, casting sidelong glances at her as they rode home, was acutely conscious of it. She was fascinating, even though she talked of things beyond his comprehension, and suddenly Baynes wanted her for himself.

That was just like Baynes. Suddenly he wanted something. The trouble was, when he wanted something he insisted on having it. That was the spoilt man in him. He thought, "She is a simple girl. I will tell her I love her and that will turn her head."

He had no thought of marriage in his mind, of course – Baynes wasn't the kind to get married. He would just have fun with the girl, and if she had a broken heart when he tired of her – well, she would get over it some day.

"Who was Korak – the white ape?" he asked suddenly. "Did he have hair all over him like other apes?" She shook her head. "Then he was a white man living in the jungle."

"Yes," she said. "A wonderful white man."

"Was he your . . . husband?" asked Baynes, a stab of jealousy unexpectedly pricking him.

"Husband?" Meriem laughed, her voice music above the sound of galloping hooves. "No, he was like a brother to me, a big brother," and with that Baynes was satisfied.

One evening he was sitting with Meriem on the veranda after the others had retired. He was telling Meriem stories of London and Paris, of balls and banquets, of the wonderful women and their wonderful gowns, of the pleasures and pastimes of the rich and powerful.

Meriem was entranced. His tales were like fairy stories to this little jungle maid. Baynes loomed large and wonderful in her mind's eye. He fascinated her, and when he drew closer to her after a short silence and took her hand she thrilled, a thrill of exaltation not unmixed with fear.

He bent his lips close to her ear.

"Meriem!" he whispered. "My little Meriem!"

The girl turned wide eyes towards his face. She trembled but did not draw away. The man put an arm about her and drew her closer.

"I love you!" he whispered.

She did not reply. She did not know what to say.

"Tell me," he said, "that you return my love."

His lips came steadily closer to hers. They had almost touched when a vision of Korak sprang before her eyes. She saw Korak's face close to hers, she felt his lips hot against her lips, and then for the first time in her life she guessed what love meant. She drew away gently.

"I am not sure," she said, "that I love you. Let us wait. There is plenty of time."

Meriem rose. The vision of Korak was still before her.

"Goodnight," she said. "It is almost too beautiful to leave." She looked round at the starry heavens, the great moon, the broad, silvered plain, and the dense shadows in the distance that marked the jungle. "Oh, how I love it!"

"You would love London more," he said earnestly. "And London would love you. You would be a famous beauty in any capital of Europe. You would have the world at your feet, Meriem."

"Goodnight!" she repeated, and left him.

Baynes selected a cigarette from his crested case, lit it, blew a thin line of blue smoke towards the moon, and smiled.

## Hanson the Trader

Meriem and Bwana were seated on the veranda the following day when a horseman appeared in the distance riding across the plain towards the bungalow. Bwana shaded his eyes with his hand and gazed towards the oncoming rider. He was puzzled. Strangers were few in

Central Africa. No white man came within a hundred miles without word of his approach reaching Bwana long before his arrival.

But here was one who had slipped into the country unheralded. Bwana could not imagine who the approaching horseman might be. He met the newcomer at the gate, welcoming him even before he had dismounted. He saw a tall, well-knit man of thirty or over, blond and smooth shaven. There was a tantalizing familiarity about him that made Bwana feel he should be able to call the visitor by name, yet he was unable to do so.

The newcomer was evidently of Scandinavian origin – both in appearance and accent. His manner was rough but open.

"It is unusual for a white man to come unheralded," Bwana said as they walked together towards the bungalow. "My friends, the natives, keep me well-posted."

"It is probably due to the fact that I came from the south," explained the stranger. "I have seen no village for several marches."

"No, there are none to the south for many miles," replied Bwana. "Since Kovudoo deserted his country I rather doubt one could find a native in that direction for two or three hundred miles."

All the same, Bwana was wondering how a lone white man could have made his way through the savage, inhospitable miles that lay to the south. As though guessing what was passing through the other's mind, the stranger offered an explanation.

"I came down from the north to do a little trading and hunting," he said, "and got away off the beaten track. My head-man, who was the only member of the *safari* who had ever been in the country before, took sick and died. We could find no natives to guide us, and so I simply swung back straight north.

"I had no idea there was a white man within a thousand miles of us when we camped last night by a waterhole at the edge of the plain. This morning I started out
103

to hunt and saw the smoke from your chimney, so I rode straight over. Of course, I've heard of you – everybody who comes into Central Africa does – and I'd be mighty glad of permission to rest up and hunt around here for a couple of weeks."

"Certainly," replied Bwana. "Move your camp close to the river below my boys' camp and make yourself at home."

They had reached the veranda now and Bwana introduced the stranger to Meriem and My Dear, who had just come from the bungalow's interior.

"This is Mr. Hanson," he said, using the name the man had given him. "He is a trader who has lost his way in the jungle to the south."

My Dear and Meriem greeted the stranger who seemed rather ill at ease in their presence. His host attributed this to the fact that his guest was unaccustomed to the society of women, and so he led him away to his study and a brandy and soda, which were evidently much less embarrassing to Mr. Hanson.

When the two had left them Meriem turned towards My Dear.

"It is odd," she said, "but I could almost swear that I had known Mr. Hanson in the past. It is odd, but quite impossible," and she gave the matter no further thought.

Hanson did not accept Bwana's invitation to move his camp closer to the bungalow. He said his boys were inclined to be quarrelsome, and so were better off at a distance. He himself was around but little, and then always avoided coming into contact with the ladies, which aroused only laughing comment on the rough trader's bashfulness.

Of an evening he often spent much time with the white foreman of the big farm, so that his was a familiar figure about the premises by night. He came and went as he saw fit, often wandering alone in the great flower garden that was the especial pride and joy of My Dear and Meriem.

For three weeks Hanson stayed. During this time he

said his boys were resting after their terrible ordeal in the untracked jungle, but he had not been as idle as he appeared to have been. He divided his small following into two parties, entrusting the leadership of each to men whom he believed he could trust.

One party he moved very slowly northward along the trail that connected with the great caravan-routes entering the Sahara from the south. The other he ordered straight westward, with orders to go into permanent camp just beyond the great river which marks the natural boundary of the country that the big Bwana rightfully considered almost his own.

To his host he explained that he was moving his *safari* slowly towards the north – he said nothing of the party moving westward.

And thus matters stood when, one hot night, Meriem, unable to sleep, rose and wandered out into the garden.

Behind a great flowering shrub Hanson lay gazing at the stars and waiting. He heard the girl approaching, and half raised himself to his elbow. A dozen paces away, the reins looped over a fence post, stood his pony.

Meriem, walking slowly, approaching the bush behind which he lay. Hanson drew a large handkerchief from his pocket and rose stealthily to his knees. A pony neighed down at the corrals. Far out across the plain a lion roared. Hanson changed his position until he squatted upon both feet, ready to come erect quickly.

Again the pony neighed – this time closer. There was the sound of its body brushing against shrubbery.

The man turned his head in the direction of the beast. What he saw sent him to the ground, huddled close beneath the shrubbery – a man was coming, leading two ponies.

Meriem heard them now and stopped to listen. A moment later Baynes drew near, two saddled mounts at his heels.

Meriem looked up at him in surprise. Baynes grinned sheepishly.

105

"I couldn't sleep," he explained, "and was going for a bit of a ride when I saw you out here, and I thought you'd like to join me."

Meriem laughed. The adventure appealed to her.

"All right," she said.

Hanson swore beneath his breath. The two led their horses from the garden to the gate. There they discovered Hanson's mount.

"Why, here's the trader's pony," remarked Baynes.

"He's probably visiting the foreman," said Meriem.

"Pretty late for him, isn't it?" Baynes said. "I'd hate to have to ride back through that jungle at night to his camp."

The distant lion roared again. Baynes shivered and glanced at the girl to note the effect of the uncanny sound upon her. She appeared not to have noticed it.

A moment later the two mounted and rode slowly across the moon-bathed plain. The girl turned her pony's head straight towards the jungle. It was the direction of the roaring of the hungry lion.

"Hadn't we better steer clear of that fellow?" suggested Baynes. "I guess you didn't hear him."

"Yes, I heard him," said Meriem cheerfully. "Let's ride over and call on him." Morison Baynes laughed uneasily.

They were riding downwind towards the jungle. The lion lay in a little grove to their right. For two nights he had not fed. For two nights and days he had gone empty, and for a long time before that he had fed only upon carrion. He was old but he was still a terrible creature of destruction.

He caught the dangerous scent tonight, but he was ravenous. He would face a dozen rifles if necessary to fill his empty belly. He circled around into the forest in order to be downwind from his victims, for should they get his scent he could not hope to overtake them. Numa was famished, but he was old and crafty.

Deep in the jungle another caught faintly the scent of

106

man and Numa. He raised his head and sniffed. He cocked it upon one side and listened.

"Come on," said Meriem, "let's ride in a little way – the forest is wonderful at night.

"You needn't be afraid of the lion," Meriem said, noting his slight hesitancy. "There hasn't been a man-eater around here for two years, Bwana says."

"Oh, I'm not afraid of lions," replied Baynes carelessly, and he urged his pony into the dark shadows of the wood. Behind him came Meriem and in front, prowling ahead and awaiting a favourable opportunity, skulked Numa the lion.

Out upon the plain a lone horseman muttered a low curse as he saw the two disappear from sight. It was Hanson. He had followed them from the bungalow.

Now he turned towards the spot where they had entered the jungle.

Meriem and Baynes had halted in a small, natural clearing. A hundred yards beyond them Numa lay crouching in the underbrush, his yellow-green eyes fixed upon his prey.

Behind him the other who had caught the scent of man and lion sat up in the tree where he had been sleeping. Beneath him a lumbering grey hulk swayed to and fro in the darkness. The thing in the tree dropped to the back of the grey mass. He whispered a word in one of the great ears and Tantor the elephant raised his trunk aloft, swinging it high and low to catch the scent that the word had warned him of. There was another whispered word and the lumbering beast wheeled into an awkward, yet silent shuffle, in the direction of Numa the lion and the stranger Tarmangani his rider had scented.

Onward they went, the scent of the lion and his prey growing stronger and stronger. Numa was becoming impatient. How much longer must he wait for his meat to come his way? He lashed his tail viciously. He almost growled. Unconscious of their danger the man and the girl sat talking in the little clearing.

Their horses were standing side by side. Baynes had found Meriem's hand and was holding it as he poured words of love into her ear, and Meriem was listening.

"Come to London with me," urged Morison Baynes. "I can gather a *safari* and we can be a whole day upon the way to the coast before they guess that we have gone."

"Why must we go that way?" asked the girl. "Bwana and My Dear would not object to our marriage."

"I cannot marry you just yet," explained Baynes. "There are some formalities to be attended to first – you do not understand. It will be all right, though. We will go to London. If you love me you will come. What do we care for anyone in the world beside ourselves? I would give my life for you – will you give nothing for me?"

"You love me?" she asked. "You will marry me when we reach London?"

"I swear it," he cried.

"I will go with you," she whispered, "though I do not understand why it is necessary." She leaned towards him and he took her in his arms and bent to press his lips to hers.

At the same instant the head of a huge tusker poked through the trees that fringed the clearing. Baynes and Meriem, with eyes and ears for one another alone, did not see or hear – but Numa did. The man upon Tantor's broad head saw the girl in the man's arms. It was Korak, but in the trim figure of the neatly dressed girl he did not recognize his Meriem. He only saw a Tarmangani with his she.

And then Numa charged.

With a frightful roar, fearful lest Tantor had come to frighten away his prey, the great beast leapt from his hiding-place. The earth trembled to his mighty voice.

Baynes went white and cold. The lion was charging towards them in the brilliant light of the magnificent moon. Baynes' muscles no longer obeyed his will – they flexed to the urge of a greater power – the power of Nature's
108

first law. They drove his spurred heels deep into the pony's flanks, forcing him towards the plain and safety.

The girl's pony, squealing in terror, reared and plunged upon the heels of his mate. The lion was close behind them. Only the girl was cool – the girl and the half-naked savage who bestrode the neck of his mighty mount and grinned at the exciting spectacle.

To Korak these were only two strange Tarmangani pursued by Numa, who was hungry. It was Numa's right to prey, but one was a she. Korak felt an instinctive urge to rush to her protection.

He ordered Tantor forward. Then he raised his heavy spear and hurled it at the flying target of the lion's body. The girl's pony had reached the trees on the opposite side of the clearing. Here he would become easy prey to the swiftly moving lion, but Numa, infuriated, preferred the woman upon his back. It was for her he leapt.

Korak gave an exclamation of astonishment as Numa landed upon the pony's rump and at the same instant the girl swung free of her mount to the branches of a tree above her.

Korak's spear struck Numa in the shoulder, knocking him from the frantically plunging horse. Freed of the weight of both girl and lion the pony raced away towards safety. Numa tore at the missile in his shoulder but could not dislodge it. Then in fury he resumed the chase.

Korak guided Tantor into the seclusion of the jungle. He did not wish to be seen.

Hanson had almost reached the wood when he heard the lion's roars, and knew that the charge had come. An instant later Baynes came into view, racing like mad for safety. An instant later the second pony appeared – rider-less.

Hanson groaned as he guessed what had happened out of sight in the jungle. With an oath he spurred on in the hope of driving the lion from his prey, his rifle ready in his hand. Then the lion came into view behind the girl's pony. Hanson could not understand. He knew that if Numa had succeeded in seizing the girl he would not have continued in pursuit of the others.

He drew in his own mount, took quick aim and fired. The lion stopped in his tracks, turned and bit at his side, then rolled over dead. Hanson rode on into the forest, calling aloud to the girl.

"Here I am," came a quick response from the foliage of the trees just ahead. "Did you hit him?"

"Yes," replied Hanson. "Where are you? You had a mighty narrow escape. It will teach you to keep out of the jungle at night."

Together they returned to the plain where they found Baynes riding slowly back towards them. He explained that his pony had bolted and that he had had difficulty in stopping him at all. Hanson grinned, for he recalled the pounding heels that he had seen driving sharp spurs into the flanks of Baynes' mount, but he said nothing. Baynes took Meriem up behind him and the three rode in silence towards the bungalow.


## Hanson's Trickery

Behind them Korak emerged from the jungle and recovered his spear from Numa's side. He was still smiling. He had enjoyed the spectacle exceedingly. There was only one thing which troubled him – the agility with which the she had clambered from her pony's back into the safety of the tree *above* her. That was more like a Mangani – more like his lost Meriem. With a sigh he turned back into the jungle.

At the bungalow Bwana met the returning adventurers on the veranda. He had heard the report of Hanson's rifle far out across the plain, and wondered what it could mean. Presently it occurred to him that Hanson might have met with an accident on his way back to camp, so he went to his foreman's quarters, where he learned that the Swede had departed several hours before.

Returning from the foreman Bwana noticed that the corral gate was open. Meriem's pony was gone and also the one used by Baynes. Instantly Bwana assumed that the shot had been fired by Baynes and roused the ranch. He was preparing to investigate when he saw a party approaching across the plain.

Explanations on the part of the Englishman met a rather chilly reception from his host. Meriem was silent. She saw that Bwana was angry with her. It was the first time, and she was heart-broken.

"Go to your room, Meriem," he said. "Baynes if you will step into my study, I'd like to have a word with you."

Bwana stepped towards Hanson as the others turned to obey him. There was something about Bwana even in his gentlest moods that commanded instant obedience.

"How did you happen to be with them, Hanson?" he asked.

"I'd been sitting in the garden," replied the trader, "after leaving Jervis' quarters. Tonight I fell asleep behind a bush, and was awakened by them two talking. I couldn't hear what they said, but presently Baynes brings two ponies and they ride off. I knew they hadn't ought to be ridin' about that time of night, leastways not the girl – it wasn't right and it wasn't safe. So I follows them, and it's just as well I did. Baynes was gettin' away from the lion as fast as he could, leavin' the girl to take care of herself, when I got a lucky shot into the beast's shoulder that fixed him."

Hanson paused. Both men were silent for a time. Presently the trader coughed in an embarrassed manner, as though there was something on his mind he felt in duty bound to say, but hated to.

"What is it, Hanson?" asked Bwana.

"Well, you see it's like this," ventured Hanson. "Bein' around here evenings a good deal I've seen them

111

two together a lot, and, beggin' your pardon, sir, but I don't think Mr. Baynes means the girl any good. I've overheard enough to make me think he's tryin' to get her to run off with him." Hanson, to fit his own ends, hit nearer the truth than he knew.

"I thought," continued the trader, "that since I'm about due to move you might like to suggest to Mr. Baynes that he go with me. I'd be willin' to take him north to the caravan trails as a favour to you, sir."

Bwana stood in deep thought for a moment. Presently he looked up.

"Of course, Hanson, Mr. Baynes is my guest," he said, a grim twinkle in his eye. "If I recall his words correctly, it seems to me he has spoken of returning home. I am sure nothing would delight him more than to go north with you. You say you start tomorrow? I think Mr. Baynes will accompany you. Drop over in the morning, if you please, and now goodnight, and thank you for keeping a watchful eye on Meriem."

Hanson hid a grin as he turned to his saddle. Bwana stepped from the veranda to his study, where he found Morison Baynes pacing back and forth, evidently ill at ease.

"Baynes," said Bwana, coming directly to the point, "Hanson is leaving for the north tomorrow. He has taken a great fancy to you, and just asked me to say he'd be glad to have you accompany him. Goodnight, Baynes."

At Bwana's suggestion Meriem kept to her room the following morning until after Morison Baynes had departed.

Bwana did not mention the subject again to her, and in this he made a mistake, for the young girl was both proud and sensitive. Bwana's action in sending Baynes away hurt her deeply. Also it did much to make a martyr of Baynes in her eyes and aroused in her breast a feeling of loyalty towards him.

As Baynes and Hanson rode towards the latter's camp the Englishman maintained a morose silence.

112

"Rough on you, wasn't he?" the Swede said suddenly, jerking his head back in the direction of the bungalow. "If I was you, I wouldn't let any man keep me from gettin' the girl I wanted. Between you and me, I ain't got no use for him and if I can help you in any way just call on me."

"It's good of you, Hanson," replied Baynes, "but what can a fellow do about it."

"I know what I'd do," said Hanson. "I'd take the girl along with me. If she loves you, she'll go all right."

"It can't be done," replied Baynes. "He bosses this whole country for miles around. He'd be sure to catch us."

"No, he wouldn't – not with me running things," said Hanson. "If you want to take the girl along I'll help you, and I'll guarantee that nobody will catch up with us before we reach the coast.

"You write her a note, and I'll get it to her by my headman. Ask her to meet you to say goodbye – she won't refuse that. In the meantime, we can be movin' camp a little farther north all the time.

"Tell her I'll meet her while you wait for us in camp. That'll be better, for I know the country well and can cover ground quicker than you. You can take charge of the *safari* and be movin' along slowly towards the north, and the girl and I'll catch up with you."

Baynes thought for a moment and then nodded quick agreement. It seemed the perfect solution. They rode on, talking together.

The sounds of their careless passage through the trees came to the ears of another jungle wayfarer. Korak had returned to the place where he had seen the white girl who took to the trees with such agility. There was something compelling in the memory of her that drew him irresistibly towards her. He wished to see her by the light of day.

Now he was moving lazily back in the direction of the spot where he had seen the girl when sounds of approaching horsemen came to his sharp ears. Stealthily he moved

113

through the branches until he came within sight of the riders. The younger man he instantly recognized as the one he had seen with his arms about the girl just before Numa charged. The other he did not recognize, though there was a familiarity about him that puzzled Korak.

The ape-man decided that to find the girl again he would need only to keep in touch with the young Englishman, and so he fell in behind the pair, following them to Hanson's camp. Here Baynes wrote a brief note, which Hanson gave into the keeping of one of his boys, who immediately started off towards the south.

Korak remained near the camp, keeping a careful watch upon the Englishmen. He had half expected to find the girl at the camp and was disappointed when there was no sign of her.

Baynes was restless, pacing back and forth beneath the trees. Hanson lay in his hammock and smoked. Korak lay stretched upon a branch among the dense foliage above them. Thus passed the rest of the afternoon.


In the garden beside the bungalow Meriem wandered in the moonlight. She still resented Bwana's treatment of Baynes, which she believed to be unjust. Nothing had been explained to her, for Bwana had wished to spare her the true explanation of Baynes' proposal. They knew, as Meriem did not, that the man had no intention of marrying her.

Meriem loved them both and was grateful to them for all they had done for her. But deep in her heart surged the savage love of liberty that years of freedom in the jungle had made part of her being. Now, for the first time, Meriem felt like a prisoner in the bungalow of Bwana and My Dear.

Like a caged tigress the girl paced the length of the garden. Once she paused near the outer fence, her head upon one side – listening. What was it she heard? The pad of naked human feet just beyond the garden? She listened

114

for a moment. The sound was not repeated. Then she resumed her restless walking.

Down to the opposite end of the garden she passed, turned and retraced her steps towards the upper end. Upon the grass near the bushes lay a white envelope that had not been there a moment before.

Meriem stooped and picked up the envelope. Tearing it open, she easily read the contents by the moon's brilliant light. It was, as she had guessed, from Baynes.

"I cannot go without seeing you again," it read. "Come to the clearing early tomorrow morning and say goodbye to me. Come alone."

There was a little more – words that made her heart beat faster and a happy flush mount her cheek.


It was still dark when Baynes set out for the meeting-place. Behind and above him, though he did not know it, came Korak, whom the noise in the camp had awakened.

It was nine o'clock before Baynes drew rein in the clearing. Meriem had not yet arrived. Korak stretched himself comfortably upon a lofty limb, where he could watch those beneath him without being seen.

An hour passed. Baynes gave evidence of nervousness. Korak had already guessed that the young Englishman had come to meet the nimble she who had so forcefully reminded him of Meriem.

Presently the sound of an approaching horse came to Korak's ears. She was coming! The foliage parted to the head and shoulders of her mount and the girl rode into view. Baynes spurred to meet her.

Korak saw the man take both her hands and draw her close to his breast. He saw the man's face concealed for a moment beneath the same broad brim that hid the girl's. He could imagine their lips meeting, and he closed his eyes for an instant in silent agony.

When he looked again they had drawn apart and were talking earnestly. Korak could see the man urging something. It was equally evident that the girl was holding back. Many of her gestures and the way she tossed her head reminded Korak still more strongly of Meriem.

And then the conversation was over and the man took the girl in his arms to kiss her goodbye. She turned and rode towards the point from which she had come. The man sat on his horse watching her. At the edge of the jungle she turned to wave him a final farewell.

"Tonight!" she cried, throwing back her head as she called to him – throwing back her head and revealing her face for the first time to the eyes of young Tarzan in the tree above.

Korak started as though pierced through the heart with an arrow. It was impossible! It could not be true! And yet with his own eyes he had seen his Meriem – more beautiful then ever, yet still his Meriem. She had not died! He had seen her – he had seen his Meriem – *in the arms of another man!* And that man sat below him now, within easy reach.

Korak fondled his heavy spear. He stroked the hunting knife at his hip. And the man beneath him bent the rein to his pony's neck, and moved off towards the north.

Still Korak sat alone among the trees. Now his hands hung idly at his sides. His weapons were forgotten for the moment. Korak was thinking.

He still loved her, and jealousy seared his soul as he recalled the sight of her in the arms of the young Englishman. His Meriem loved another! For a long time he let that awful truth sink deep, and from it he tried to reason out his future.

In his heart was a great desire to follow the man and slay him, but always there came the thought – she loves him. Could he slay the man that Meriem loved? He shook his head.

Next came an impulse to follow Meriem and speak with her. He half started, and then glanced down at his nakedness and was ashamed. He, the son of a British peer, had thrown away his life, had reduced himself to the level of a beast so that he was ashamed to go to the woman he loved and lay his love at her feet. For what had he to offer her?

In her new world she loved a man of her own kind. And Korak knew that it was right. She was not for him – not for the naked, savage ape. No, she was not for him – but he still was hers! If he could not have her and happiness, he would at least do all that lay in his power to assure happiness for her. He would follow the young Englishman and, though jealousy wrenched his heart, he would watch over the man Meriem loved, for Meriem's sake.

And so it happened that a few minutes after Baynes entered the camp, to be greeted by Hanson, Korak again slipped noiselessly into a nearby tree. There he lay until late afternoon, and still the young Englishman made no move to leave camp. Korak wondered if Meriem were coming there. A little later Hanson and one of the natives rode out of camp. Korak merely noted the fact. He was not particularly interested.

Darkness came, and still the young man remained. He ate his evening meal, afterwards smoking numerous cigarettes. Presently he began to pace back and forth before his tent. A lion coughed and he went into his tent, to reappear with an express rifle. He ordered the boy to throw more brush upon the fire. Korak saw that he was nervous and afraid, and his lip curled in a sneer of contempt.

Hanson and his boy had ridden directly to the clearing. It was already dark when they arrived. Leaving the boy there, Hanson rode to the edge of the plain, leading the boy's horse. There he waited. It was nine o'clock before he saw a solitary figure galloping towards him from the direction of the bungalow. A few moments later Meriem drew in her mount beside him. She was nervous and

117

flushed. When she recognized Hanson she drew back, startled.

"Mr. Baynes' horse fell on him and sprained his ankle," Hanson hastened to explain. "He couldn't very well come, so he sent me to bring you to camp."

In the darkness the girl could not see the gloating, triumphant expression on the speaker's face.

"We had better hurry," continued Hanson, "for we'll have to move along pretty fast if we don't want to be overtaken."

"Is he hurt badly?" asked Meriem.

"Only a little sprain," replied Hanson. "He can ride all right."

Hanson swung his pony round and Meriem followed him. They rode north along the edge of the jungle for a mile, and then turned towards the west. Meriem, following, paid little attention to their direction. She did not know where Hanson's camp lay, and she did not guess that he was not leading her towards it.

All night they rode, straight towards the west. When morning came, Hanson permitted a short halt for breakfast. Then they pushed on again, nor did they halt a second time until in the heat of the day he stopped and motioned the girl to dismount.

"We will sleep here for a time and let the ponies graze," he said.

"I had no idea the camp was so far away," said Meriem.

"I left orders that they were to move at daybreak," explained the trader. "It may not be until tomorrow that we catch up with them."

But though they travelled part of the night and all the following day no sign of the *safari* appeared ahead. Meriem, an adept in jungle craft, knew that none had passed ahead of them for many days.

At last she became suspicious. Gradually the attitude of the man at her side had begun to change. She became more certain that somewhere, sometime before, she had known this man. He had not shaved for several days. A blond stubble began to cover his chin, and with it the feeling that he was no stranger continued to grow upon the girl.

It was not until the second day, however, that Meriem rebelled. She drew in her pony at last and voiced her doubts. Hanson assured her that the camp was only a few miles farther on.

"We should have overtaken them yesterday," he said. "They must have marched much faster than I had believed possible."

"They have not marched here at all," said Meriem. "The spoor that we have been following is weeks old."

Hanson laughed.

"Oh, that's it, is it?" he cried. "Why didn't you say so before? I could have easily explained it. We are not coming by the same route, but we'll pick up their trail sometime today, even if we don't overtake them."

Now at last Meriem knew that the man was lying to her. She said nothing, however, planning to escape at the first opportunity.

She watched his face continually without being observed. Where had she known him? When had they met before?

She ran over in her mind the few white men she had known. There were some who had come to her father's *douar* in the jungle. Ah, now she had it! She had seen him there, yet still for the moment she could not remember who he was.

It was mid-afternoon when suddenly they broke out of the jungle onto the banks of a broad and a placid river. On the opposite side Meriem could see a camp surrounded by a high thorn *boma*.

At a shout from Hanson the natives in the camp ran down to the river bank and launched a big canoe to bring the Swede and his party across. The horses were left behind to be picked up on the second trip.

Meriem wondered if Hanson had been telling the truth

119

all along. Was Baynes really waiting for her here? The camp certainly existed as he had promised. She spoke to Hanson, that blond, vaguely familiar Swede.

"Where is Morison?" The words were curt but there was a tremor in her voice. Now she distrusted the man. Hanson pointed towards the tent which stood alone in the centre of the camp.

"There," he said and walked towards it with her. At the entrance he held the flap open and gestured her inside. Meriem entered and looked round. The tent was empty. Empty except for a long stake driven deep into the ground and a slave chain!

Horrified she turned to Hanson. Suddenly recognition came! She knew the man. It was Malbihn, the ruthless and brutal Swede from whom Bwana had rescued her.

As he advanced upon her now, though, a cruel glint in his eye, she knew well that today there would be no Bwana to save her. A river and miles of jungle separated her from her friends.


Morison Baynes had spent a sleepless night in the camp of the Swede. Pacing to and fro he had waited for the arrival of his partner and Meriem. Meriem! How he longed to see her again, to hold her in his arms once more. But mingled with the thoughts of Meriem was fear of his former host, the Big Bwana as the natives called him.

Suppose that he had surprised Hanson making off with the girl? He might even now be on his way north to punish him, and the Bwana was a law unto himself in this part of Africa. Baynes shuddered at the thought of what might happen to the man who got on the wrong side of the Bwana.

It was morning now and he leapt to his feet. There was no sign of Hanson and time was creeping on. The night had only increased his fears. He decided to get out of the Bwana's territory now and travel north with all possible
120

speed. If Hanson had been captured, each moment he stayed made his own chances of escape slimmer.

He ordered the headman to break camp immediately, and stood there anxiously watching the natives work. Constantly he looked over his shoulder, every moment expecting to see the tall figure of Bwana stride into view.

Within the hour the *safari* was moving rapidly northwards. It was noon when they came upon a tired and sweat-covered runner. He was greeted with shouts of recognition from the trudging column, who came to a halt and listened to his story.

It was the boy who had left the camp with Hanson and been deserted by the Swede before the latter met Meriem. He had hated his master for years, and only fear had tied him to the Swede – fear of the man's whip and his ever-present gun.

Finally realising that he had been abandoned in the jungle he had decided to seek out his friends in the north camp.

The boy was cheerful now that he was with his old companions, and it made him incautious. He began to tell of what he knew and spoke loudly and in his best English and standing not far away Baynes was able to overhear him.

He told of pony tracks which he had discovered on his return journey. One, he knew, belonged to the white missie. These tracks and Hanson's had gone west towards the other camp on the river. Hanson was running away with the white missie, the boy laughed loudly, delighted by intrigue and cunning even though he hated his white master.

Standing there, letting it all sink in, Baynes began to understand. Hanson had not brought the girl back to the camp as he had promised. Hanson was taking her to the other camp. That could only mean one thing – Hanson was double-crossing him!

Anger began to build up in Baynes at that. First it was against Hanson for his treachery, then curiously it began

121

to be directed towards himself. All at once Baynes was aghast. All at once he realized that he was genuinely fond of Meriem – he had pretended to be in love with her and now he realized he had truly fallen in love with the beautiful jungle maiden.

A feeling of frantic anxiety rose in him. Meriem was in the power of this man Hanson, a man who did not inspire Baynes with confidence in any way. Poor Meriem – and he was responsible for her plight.

It was at that moment that a change came over the playboy, Baynes. This man who feared the jungle, who had no courage where physical things were concerned, from that moment became recklessly indifferent to danger and hardship in his concern to right the wrong he had done to an innocent girl.

Abruptly he called the boy to him. The boy came forward, somewhat cheekily, for he and his companions had only contempt for Baynes. But his manner changed when he saw Baynes standing there, grim-eyed and determined.

"You know where the west camp is?"

"Yes, bwana."

"Take me to it. We start at once."

Baynes turned to his horse. A few minutes later both were riding out of the camp. It was the beginning of the most awful journey Baynes had ever undertaken, something so terrible that there were times when he wanted to abandon it, and yet love for Meriem drove him on.

They rode until the way was too rough for their horses, and then they took to foot. They marched on, through prickly jungle, through hot and steaming swampland where snakes and crocodiles were extra hazards to their passage.

They went as fast as they could go until it was too dark to proceed, and then they slept in the branches of a tree – uneasily, fitfully, and when morning came they were so stiff they could hardly stir their limbs.

On again, fighting their way through thick jungle,

122

climbing a mountain that day, going the shortest but the hardest way in order to save time. Scratched and bleeding, their clothing torn to ribbons, they rarely stopped for rest and food. And all the time the heat of the African jungle was on them, merciless, murderous.

When he had given up hope of ever breaking through the jungle, miraculously they found the river. Bleeding and staggering from fatigue, Baynes and the native followed its course upstream until they came in sight of the camp on the opposite bank.

And they were just in time. Even as they saw the camp, they saw a broad ferry boat being poled across, and on it were three horses. It was far away, but Baynes even thought he could distinguish Meriem standing with them.

Now they began to search for a boat, and finally found an old, half-submerged canoe drawn up the bank. They baled it out, found some pieces of wood and began to pole and paddle their way across.

Suddenly they were seen by the bearers in the west camp, and they came down to the river to call to them. Hanson was in the tent. The shouts brought him out in a hurry. He swore as he saw Baynes paddling towards him. He strode down to the edge of the river and shouted, "What do you want?" though he knew.

"You, you treacherous devil!" shouted Baynes, and whipping out his revolver in his rage he fired at Hanson.

Hanson levelled his rifle. His natives fled in alarm. Two shots rang out, viciously. One hit the boy who rose in agony, then pitched silently into the river. The other hit Baynes who crumpled under the impact and lay still for a moment in the bottom of the canoe.

Slowly Baynes lifted his revolver. Hanson caught the movement too late. The revolver fired. The grim smile abruptly vanished from Hanson's bearded lips. He was hit and sagged to his knees, then crumpled on his face. He was hurt – badly – but could still fire. Slowly he pushed the rifle before him, laboriously sighted it and fired. Baynes was hit again.

The canoe drifted slowly downstream. Baynes slowly, wearily, pulled himself up off the bottom of the dugout. He steadied his hand and fired and saw Hanson twitch as the heavy bullet hit him.

Hanson, even more slowly now sighted his rifle and fired. Wood splintered off the edge of the canoe. Just as slowly Baynes took aim and fired. Hanson was hit again.

In the background the natives watched in awe as the white men fought their fantastic duel.

First Hanson would fire, then after an interval Baynes' revolver would bark. Hanson was too wounded to move off the bank. Baynes could only lie out there in the stream, the canoe poor protection for him.

Each was hit twice again, though not severely now – their aim was getting worse. Finally the canoe drifted round a bend and the macabre duel ceased.


Meriem, chained to the stake in the tent, could only stand and listen to the ragged exchange of shots, in agony, wondering what it meant – dreading what would happen to her when Malbihn returned, as she was sure he would.

Who was firing at Malbihn? Could it be Bwana – or Korak? Hope came to her, and then dread followed as she heard more firing. She moved. To her astonishment the collar sagged open round her neck. In his haste to get outside, Malbihn had bungled the locking of the clumsv old slave collar. She was free!

She saw Malbihn's revolver lying on a case. With trembling fingers she took the gun then slipped outside. No one was watching. Everyone was staring at Malbihn, lying on his face, his gun silent. She looked at the river. No one was in sight.

Meriem took hold of herself. She looked at the revolver. It was unloaded. An unloaded gun was no good

124

to her if she was to flee through the jungle. She opened the case. There was ammunition inside. With hurried fingers she loaded the gun.

And then she saw something – something lying carelessly in amid the ammunition. There were some letters wrapped round with a piece of tape, and on top, staring up at her, was a photograph.

Something about it was familiar so that even in her haste she paused to pick it up. It was a newspaper cutting, yellowed with age, but the picture was remarkably clear. It was the face of a little girl and the face of the girl struck a chord – it was familiar. All at once Meriem realized that she was looking at herself, a picture taken years ago. She took it out of the bundle and examined it for a brief moment. There were printed words under the picture, but Meriem could not read them, did not know what they had to say. They were in French.

A sound outside. Instantly Meriem was alert. Pushing the newspaper cutting inside her blouse, she slipped outside again. Alongside the tent, very conveniently a branch of a tree overhung the *boma*. Meriem leapt – a leap no ordinary girl could have accomplished – caught the branch and in seconds was over the prickly *boma*.

For a moment she hesitated, about to plunge into the forest. Then reason came to her. Her friends were across the river. In some way she had to get across; it was no good continuing her flight westward.

Some distance away were canoes, drawn up on the shore. Desperately Meriem ran to them, and luck was on her side. No one saw her. She pushed off and began to paddle – and still no shout came to tell her she had been seen. She was half-way across the river before anyone looked up and then it was the native boys and they only pointed and shouted and did nothing more than that.

So Meriem paddled on, hopefully towards freedom. And ahead of her eyes watched and the eyes were grim and merciless – many eyes. Meriem was running into a danger as great as if she'd been with Malbihn.

She made the far bank and leapt ashore. Here she found herself on the edge of an abandoned native village, the huts crumbling into decay, silent and ruined in the sun.

Meriem began to run through the village. From dark doorways those hard, merciless eyes watched her. All at once a shout went out, sharp, imperative – an order. Instantly a flood of white-robed Arabs came pouring out of the decayed dwellings. Meriem screamed, shocked by the suddenness of their appearance. Hands grasped her. She was helpless, once more a prisoner.

A man came forward, rather more richly dressed than the others. She saw the thin, cruel face and moaned. It was her father, The Sheik!

All her childhood fears returned in that awful moment. She could only look into that terrifying face and wish she was dead.

The Sheik spoke, his voice rasping. "So you have come back!"

"Let me go!" she implored. "Let me go back to the Big Bwana!"

"The Big Bwana? Is that where you have been all this time? Was it the Big Bwana who took you from me?"

Meriem took courage. "The Big Bwana is my friend. He will be following me. If you harm me he will kill you!" Unexpectedly she laughed in her "father's" face.

The shot went home. There was only one man The Sheik feared, and that was the Big Bwana. Hurriedly he gave an order and the party moved off.

Across the river Malbihn's boys watched it all happen, and when the Arabs passed out of sight they reported to their master.

The Sheik and his party had been marching southward along the river when one of them had seen Meriem paddling desperately from the opposite shore. The fellow had called The Sheik's attention to the strange sight – a white woman alone in Central Africa. The old Arab had hidden his men in the deserted village to capture her when she landed, for thoughts of ransom were always in the mind of The Sheik.

When at last the woman walked into the trap he had set for her, and he recognized her as the same girl he had maltreated years before, his pleasure was enormous.

Now he lost no time in establishing the old relationship of father and daughter that had existed between them in the past. At the first opportunity he struck her a heavy blow across the face. He seemed to revel in the discovery of new methods of torturing or humiliating her, and among all his followers she found no one who dared to defend her.

A two days' march brought them at last to the familiar scenes of her childhood. And the first face upon which she set her eyes as she was driven through the gates into the strong stockade was that of the toothless, hideous Mabunu, her one-time nurse. It was as though all the years that had intervened were but a dream.

Among the Arabs who had come to the village in her absence was a tall young fellow of twenty – a handsome, sinister-looking youth – who stared at her in open admiration until The Sheik ordered him away. Abdul Kamak went, scowling.

At last Meriem was alone. As of old, she was permitted the freedom of the village, for the stockade was high and strong and the only gates were well guarded by day and night.

And so, as she had done in the sad days of her childhood, she slunk down to an unfrequented corner of the enclosure where she had often played beneath the great tree that had overhung the palisade. But now the tree was gone, and Meriem guessed the reason. It was from this tree that Korak had descended and struck down The Sheik when he had rescued her from the misery and torture that had filled her early years.

A glow of happiness warmed her heart as she recalled

127

her first meeting with Korak and then the long years that he had cared for her. For months Korak had not occupied her thoughts as he did today. He seemed closer and dearer now than ever before.

Then came the image of Morison, and Meriem was troubled. Did she really love the young Englishman?

Meriem pressed her hand above her heart as she stifled a sigh, and as she did so she felt the soft outlines of the photograph. Now she drew it forth and re-examined it more carefully.

She was sure the baby face was her own. She studied every detail of the picture. Half-hidden in the dainty dress rested a chain and locket. Meriem puckered her brows. What tantalizing half-memories it awakened! Could this flower of civilization be the little Arab Meriem, daughter of The Sheik? It was impossible, and yet that locket? Meriem knew it.

She had seen that locket before, and it had been hers. What strange mystery lay buried in her past?

As she sat gazing at the picture she became suddenly aware that she was not alone – that someone was standing close behind her – someone who had approached her noiselessly. Guiltily she thrust the picture back into her blouse. A hand fell upon her shoulder. She was sure it was The Sheik, and she awaited in dumb terror the blow that would follow.

No blow came, and she looked upward over her shoulder into the eyes of Abdul Kamak, the young Arab.

"I saw," he said, "the picture that you have just hidden. It is you when you were a child – a very young child. May I see it again?"

Meriem drew away from him.

"I will give it back," he said. "I have heard of you, and I know you have no love for The Sheik, your father. Neither have I. I will not betray you. Let me see the picture."

Friendless among cruel enemies, Meriem clutched at

the possibility of an ally. She drew the photograph from its hiding-place and handed it to him.

Abdul Kamak examined it carefully. Slowly he nodded.

"Yes," he said, "it is you, but where was it taken?"

"I do not know," replied Meriem. "I never saw the picture until a couple of days ago, when I found it in the tent of the Swede, Malbihn."

Abdul Kamak raised his eyebrows. He turned the picture over, and his eyes fell upon the old newspaper cutting. He could read French and now he put his learning to use. Slowly, laboriously he read the yellow cutting. His eyes narrowed to two slits of cunning. When he had finished he looked at the girl.

"You have read this?" he asked.

"It is French," she replied, "and I do not read French."

Abdul Kamak stood in silence looking at the girl. She was very beautiful. At last he dropped to one knee beside her. A wonderful idea had occurred to him.

"Meriem," he whispered. "You do not know me, but I ask that you trust me. I hate The Sheik. Let me take you away. Come with me, and we will go back to the great desert where my father is a sheik mightier than yours."

"You hate The Sheik?" came a grim voice from behind them. "And what is that picture?"

Both turned to see The Sheik standing a few paces away. Abdul still held the picture in his hand. Now he thrust it inside his burnous.

"Yes," he said, "I hate The Sheik!" As he spoke he sprang towards the older man, felled him with a blow and dashed to where his horse stood saddled.

Leaping into the saddle, Abdul Kamak galloped for the village gates. The Sheik staggered to his feet, shouting lustily to his followers to stop the escaping Arab. A dozen men leapt to intercept the horseman, only to be ridden down or brushed aside.

With a wild whoop of exultation Abdul Kamak galloped out of the village and was swallowed up by the jungle.

Foaming with rage, The Sheik ordered immediate pursuit, and then turned back to Meriem.

"The picture!" he cried. "Where is it? Give it to me at once!"

"He took it," replied Meriem dully.

"What was it?" again demanded The Sheik, seizing the girl roughly by the hair and dragging her to her feet. "What was it a picture of?"

"Of me," said Meriem, "when I was a little girl. I stole it from Malbihn, the Swede – it had printing on the back cut from an old newspaper."

The Sheik went white with rage.

"What said the printing?" he asked in a voice so low that she barely caught his words.

"I do not know. It was in French and I cannot read French."

The Sheik seemed relieved. He almost smiled as he turned and strode away.

And along the caravan trail galloped Abdul Kamak towards the north.


As his canoe drifted out of sight of the wounded Swede Baynes sank weakly to its bottom, where he lay for long hours in a coma.

It was night before he fully regained consciousness, and then he lay for a long time looking up at the stars trying to recollect where he was.

After a while he realized that he was floating down a great African river in a native canoe – alone, wounded, and lost.

Painfully he dragged himself to a sitting position. He noticed that his wounds pained him less than he had expected. He felt them gingerly – they had ceased to bleed. Possibly they were only flesh wounds after all, and nothing serious.

From his own troubles his mind turned to Meriem's. Even if Hanson died of his wounds, would Meriem be any better off? She was in the power of equally villainous men – the brutal savages of Hanson's *safari*.

Baynes buried his face in his hands as the hideous picture of her fate burned itself into his consciousness. And it was he who had brought it upon her!

His one thought now was to atone for his selfish folly. He looked towards the shore. Dimly through the darkness of the moonless night he saw the awful blackness of the jungle, yet it did not frighten him now as it had done in the past. He did not even wonder that he was unafraid, for his mind was entirely occupied with thoughts of another's danger.

Drawing himself to his knees he leaned over the side of the canoe and started to paddle vigorously with his open palm. Though it tired and hurt him he kept at his self-imposed labour for a long time. Little by little the drifting canoe moved nearer the shore. Baynes could hear a lion roaring, so close that he felt he must be almost to the shore. He drew his rifle nearer to his side, but he did not cease to paddle.

After what seemed to the tired man an eternity he felt the brush of branches against the canoe. A moment later he reached out and clutched a leafy limb. Again the lion roared – very near it seemed now, and Baynes wondered if the brute could have been following along the shore waiting for him to land.

He tested the strength of the limb to which he clung. It seemed strong enough to support a dozen men. Then he reached down and lifted his rifle from the bottom of the canoe, slipping the sling over his shoulder. Again he tested the branch and then drew himself painfully and slowly upward until his feet swung clear of the canoe. Released, it floated silently from beneath him, to be lost for ever in the dark shadows downstream.

He had burned his bridges behind him. He must either climb aloft or drop back into the river. He struggled to raise one leg over the limb, but found himself scarcely equal to the effort, for he was very weak. For a time he hung there, feeling his strength ebbing. He knew that he must gain the branch above at once or it would be too late.

Suddenly the lion roared almost in his ear. Baynes glanced up. He saw two spots of flame a short distance above him. The lion was standing on the bank of the river glaring at him, and – waiting for him. Well, thought Baynes, let him wait. Lions can't climb trees, and if I get into this one I shall be safe enough.

The young Englishman's feet hung almost touching the surface of the water – closer than he knew, for all was pitch dark below him. Presently he heard a slight stir in the river beneath him, and something banged against one of his feet, followed almost instantly by a terrifying sound – the click of great jaws snapping together.

"By George!" exclaimed Baynes, aloud. "The beggar nearly got me." Immediately he struggled again to climb to safety, but with that final effort he knew that it was futile. He felt his tired, numbed fingers slipping from their hold – he was dropping back into the river – into the jaws of the frightful death that awaited him there.

And then he heard the leaves above him rustle to the movement of a creature among them. The branch to which he clung bent beneath an added weight. But still Baynes clung desperately – he would not give up voluntarily either to the death above or the death below.

Then he felt a soft, warm pad upon the fingers of one of his hands and then something reached down out of the blackness and dragged him up among the branches of the tree.

132

Sometimes lolling upon Tantor's back, sometimes roaming the jungle in solitude, Korak made his way slowly towards the west and south. He made only a few miles a day, for he had a whole lifetime before him and no place in particular to go.

Thus he came upon the trail of The Sheik's band as it travelled down river after capturing Meriem. Korak knew who it was that had passed, for there were few in the great jungle with whom he was not familiar. He had no particular business however, with the old Sheik, and so he did not attempt to follow him – the farther from men he could stay the better pleased he would be.

The river suggested fishing, and so he dawdled upon its shores, catching fish and eating them raw. When night came he curled up in a great tree beside the stream – the one from which he had been fishing during the afternoon – and was soon asleep.

Numa roaring beneath him, awoke him. He was about to call out in anger to his noisy neighbour when something else caught his attention. He listened. Suddenly he heard the click of a crocodile's jaws in the water beneath and then, low but distinct: "By George! The beggar nearly got me." The voice was familiar.

Korak glanced down towards the speaker. Outlined against the faint luminosity of the water he saw the figure of a man clinging to a lower branch of the tree. Silently and swiftly the ape-man clambered down. He felt a hand beneath his foot. He reached down and clutched the figure beneath him and dragged it up among the branches. Numa was still roaring beneath them, angry because he had been robbed of his prey.

Baynes felt certain that a gorilla had seized him. He felt for his revolver and was drawing it stealthily from its holster when a voice asked in perfectly good English, "Who are you?"

Baynes started so that he nearly fell from the branch. "Great Heavens!" he exclaimed. "Are you a man?"

"What did you think I was?" asked Korak.

"A gorilla," replied Baynes honestly.

Korak laughed.

"Who are you?" he repeated.

"I'm an Englishman by the name of Baynes, but who the devil are you?" asked Baynes.

"They call me The Killer," replied Korak. "You are the man I saw kissing the girl at the edge of the great plain when the lion charged you."

"Yes," said Baynes. "The girl was stolen — I am trying to rescue her."

"Stolen!" The word shot out like a bullet from a gun. "Who stole her?"

"The Swede trader, Hanson," replied Baynes.

"Where is he?"

Baynes told Korak everything that had happened since he had come upon Hanson's camp. Before he was done the first grey dawn relieved the darkness. Korak made the Englishman comfortable in the tree. He filled Baynes' canteen from the river and fetched him fruit to eat. Then he bade him goodbye.

"I am going to the Swede's camp," he announced. "I will bring the girl back to you here."

"I shall go too," insisted Baynes. "It is my right and my duty, for she was to have become my wife."

Korak winced. "You are wounded. You could not make the trip," he said. "I can go much faster alone."

"Go, then," replied Baynes, "but I shall follow."

"As you will," replied Korak, with a shrug.

And so Korak set out rapidly towards the north, and limping slowly and painfully behind him came the tired and wounded Baynes. Korak reached the river-bank opposite Malbihn's camp before Baynes had covered two miles.

Late in the afternoon the Englishman was still plodding wearily along when he heard the sound of a galloping horse behind him. Instinctively he withdrew into the underbrush, and a moment later a white-robed Arab hurtled by. Baynes did not hail the rider. He had heard of the cruel and rapacious nature of the Arabs hereabouts and was taking no chances.

When Abdul Kamak passed out of sight towards the north, Baynes resumed his weary march. A half-hour later he was again surprised by the unmistakable sound of galloping horses. This time he was caught in the open as a band of white-robed horsemen dashed into view behind him.

At sight of him they shouted in Arabic and then closed about him, threatening and angry. The leader ordered two of his men to seize and disarm him. They then placed him on the rump of one of the horses, and the two who had been detailed to guard him turned and rode back towards the south, while the others continued their pursuit of Abdul Kamak.

As Korak came out upon the bank of the river opposite the camp of Malbihn, he did not know how he could cross. He could see men moving about inside the *boma* – evidently Hanson was still there.

How was he to cross? Not even he would dare the perils of the river – almost certain death. For a moment he thought, then wheeled and sped away into the jungle, uttering a peculiar cry, shrill and piercing. Now and again he halted to listen as though for an answer to his weird call, then on again, deeper and deeper into the wood.

At last his listening ears were rewarded by the trumpeting of a bull elephant. A few moments later Korak broke through the trees into the presence of Tantor, standing with upraised trunk, waving his great ears.

"Quick, Tantor!" shouted the ape-man, and the beast swung him to his head. "Hurry!" and the mighty pachyderm lumbered off through the jungle.

Korak guided his huge mount northward to the river

a mile or more above the Swede's camp, at a point where Korak knew there was an elephant ford. Never pausing, the ape-man urged the beast into the river, and with trunk held high Tantor forged steadily towards the opposite bank. And so, in safety, they made the opposite shore, Korak perched high and dry above the turgid flood.

Then back towards the south Tantor moved, steadily and relentlessly. At last they came to the camp of the renegade Swede, but even then they did not hesitate or halt.

At a word from the ape-man, and raising his tender trunk high above the thorns, Tantor breasted the *boma*, walking through it as though it did not exist. A dozen natives squatting before their huts looked up at the noise of his approach. With sudden howls of terror they leapt to their feet and fled for the open gates.

Malbihn lay in a hammock in front of his tent. His wounds were painful and he had lost much blood. He was very weak. He looked up in surprise as he heard the screams of his men, and saw them running towards the gate. And then from around the corner of his tent loomed a huge bulk and Tantor towered above him.

The elephant stopped a couple of paces from the wounded man's hammock. Malbihn cowered, moaning. He was too weak to escape. He could only lie there gazing in horror into the blood-rimmed, angry little orbs fixed upon him, and await his death.

Then, to his astonishment, a man slid to the ground from the elephant's back. Almost at once Malbihn recognized the strange figure.

It was the white warrior who had freed the king baboon and led the angry horde of hairy devils against him and Jenssen. Malbihn cowered still lower.

"Where is the girl?" demanded Korak, in English.

"What girl?" asked Malbihn. "There is no girl here."

"The white girl," replied Korak. "Do not lie to me —

136

you lured her from her friends. You have her. Where is she?"

Malbihn shrank from the anger in the other's face.

"I will tell you," he cried. "Do not harm me, and I will tell you all I know. I had the girl here, but it was Baynes who persuaded her to leave her friends – he had promised to marry her. He does not know who she is, but I do, and I know there is a great reward for whoever takes her back to her people. It was only the reward I wanted. But she escaped and crossed the river in one of my canoes. I followed her, but The Sheik was there, God knows how, and he captured her and attacked me and drove me back. If you want her, go to The Sheik and ask him for her – she has passed as his daughter since childhood."

"She is not The Sheik's daughter?" asked Korak.

"She is not," replied Malbihn.

"Who is she, then?" asked Korak.

Here Malbihn saw his chance.

"When you find her I will tell you," he said, "if you will promise to spare my life and divide the reward with me. If you kill me, you will never know, for only The Sheik knows, and he will never tell. The girl herself is ignorant of her parentage."

"If you have told me the truth, I will spare you," said Korak. "I shall go now to The Sheik's village, and if the girl is not there I will return and kill you. As for the other information you have, if the girl wants it when we have found her, we will find a way to get it from you."

Then Korak stepped into the Swede's tent to ensure that Meriem was not hidden there. As he disappeared from view Tantor, his eyes fixed upon Malbihn, took a step nearer the man. Now he advanced his snake-like trunk towards the Swede, who shrank still deeper into his hammock.

The sensitive member felt along the body of the terrified Malbihn. Tantor uttered a low, rumbling sound. His little eyes blazed. At last he recognized the creature

137

who had killed his mate long years before. Tantor, the elephant, never forgets and never forgives. Malbihn saw murder in Tantor's eyes.

He shrieked aloud to Korak. "Help! Help! The devil is going to kill me!"

Korak ran from the tent just in time to see the enraged elephant's trunk encircle the Swede and then hammock, canopy, and man were swung high above Tantor's head. Korak leapt before the animal, commanding him to put down his prey unharmed, but his words were ignored.

Tantor wheeled round, hurled Malbihn to the earth, and knelt upon him with the quickness of a cat. Then he gored the prostrate thing through and through with his mighty tusks, trumpeting and roaring in his rage. Finally he lifted the shapeless clay that had been Sven Malbihn far aloft and hurled the bloody mass, still entangled in canopy and hammock, over the *boma* and out into the jungle.

Korak stood looking sorrowfully on at the tragedy he gladly would have averted. He had no love for the Swede, but he would have preserved the man for the sake of the secret he possessed. Now that secret was gone forever, unless The Sheik could be made to divulge it.

The ape-man, entirely unafraid of the mighty Tantor, signalled the beast to approach and lift him to its head, and Tantor came as he was bid and hoisted Korak tenderly aloft.

From the safety of their hiding-places in the jungle Malbihn's boys had witnessed the killing of their master. Now, with wide, frightened eyes, they saw the strange white warrior, mounted upon the head of his ferocious charger, disappear into the jungle.

The Sheik glowered at the prisoner whom his two men brought back from the north.

"What are you doing poaching in my country?" demanded The Shiek, instantly unpleasant and offensive.

Baynes said dryly, "I didn't know you owned this part of Africa." He was feeling very tired and weak, but somehow his mind willed him into strength and he faced the Arab unflinchingly, refusing to be intimidated by the old rogue.

After a pause he said, "When your men seized me, I was searching for a girl who had been kidnapped."

A nasty smile crossed the Sheik's face. He pointed towards the stockade wall. "That one?" he asked.

Baynes followed the direction of the bony finger. Meriem was sitting there, her back towards him.

Baynes was startled. He shouted, "Meriem!" and she turned. Baynes would have gone to her but was held back.

"What do you want with my daughter?" asked The Sheik smoothly.

"Your ... daughter!" That was too much for Baynes. This lovely girl was the daughter of a villainous Arab!

Suddenly The Sheik lost interest in Baynes. There would be time enough to think of him later – perhaps there would be ransom to be earned through the English dog. He gave an order in Arabic, and Baynes found himself seized and hurled into a hut, a sentry taking up his position outside immediately. Some time later an Arab came and bound his wrists and ankles.

Baynes lay on the floor for a long time, his wounds hurting him so much he thought he was going to pass out. Then he began to recover a little and to consider the

139

plight he was in – and Meriem's, too. He had no doubt that the girl, whether she was The Sheik's daughter or not, was not voluntarily here in the village.

He tried to loosen his bonds, but he seemed to have no strength now. Night came, and with them came rats – huge things that crawled over him and bit his ears.

Somehow he struggled to his feet, sweat pouring from him. Then he heard voices and one was a woman's and he thought it was Meriem's. He thought, "If only Meriem could untie me." Then they might escape together.

At the bungalow he had often heard Meriem sing God Save the King, as My Dear accompanied her on the piano. Raising his voice, he now hummed the tune. Immediately he heard Meriem's voice from the tent. She spoke rapidly.

"Goodbye, Morison," she cried. "If God is good I shall be dead before morning, for if I still live I shall be worse than dead after tonight."

Then he heard an angry exclamation in a man's voice, followed by the sounds of a scuffle. Baynes went white with horror. He struggled frantically with his bonds. They were giving. A moment later one hand was free. It was the work of an instant only to untie the other. He tore the rope from his ankles, then started for the doorway, bent on reaching Meriem's side. As he stepped out into the night a huge Negro rose and barred his way.


When speed was required Korak depended upon his own muscles, so the moment Tantor landed him safely on the same side of the river as the village of The Sheik, the ape-man deserted his bulky comrade and took to the trees. It was dark when he came to the palisade.

No longer did the giant tree reach over the wooden rampart, but ordinary man-made defences were nothing to Korak. Loosening the rope at his waist, he tossed the noose over one of the sharpened posts of the palisade. A moment later he was looking over the top. There was no one in sight, so Korak drew himself up and dropped lightly to the ground within the enclosure.

Then he began a stealthy search of the village. The sound of laughter fell upon his ears, and then from the opposite side of the village came the notes of a once familiar tune: God Save the King.

Korak halted in perplexity. Who could it be? The tones were those of a man. He recalled the young Englishman he had left on the river trail. A moment later there came a woman's voice in reply – it was Meriem's! Korak, spurred into action, glided rapidly in the direction of the two voices.


The evening meal over, Meriem had gone to her pallet in the woman's quarters of The Sheik's tent, a little corner screened off by a couple of priceless Persian rugs. She dwelt here with Mabunu, for The Sheik had no wives. She and Mabunu were alone now.

"Meriem!" he called. "Come here."

The girl rose and came to the front of the tent. There the light of the fire illuminated the interior. She saw Ali ben Kadin, The Sheik's half-brother, squatting on a rug, smoking. The Sheik was standing.

Ali ben Kadin was old and hideous. His nose and part of one cheek were eaten away by disease. He looked up and grinned as Meriem entered.

The Sheik jerked his thumb towards Ali ben Kadin and addressed Meriem.

"I am getting old," he said. "I shall not live much longer. Therefore I have given you to Ali ben Kadin, my brother."

That was all. Ali ben Kadin rose and came towards her. Meriem shrank back, horrified. The man seized her wrist.

"Come!" he commanded, and dragged her from The Sheik's tent and to his own.

After they had gone The Sheik chuckled. "When I send her north in a few months," he said to himself, "they

141

will know the reward for slaying the son of Amor ben Khatour!' "

In Ali ben Kadin's tent Meriem pleaded but all to no avail. The hideous old Arab spoke soft words at first, but when Meriem made her loathing clear he became enraged and seized her in his arms.

Twice she tore away from him. It was at this moment that she heard Baynes' voice humming the tune she knew was meant for her ears. At her reply Ali ben Kadin dragged her into the rear apartment of his tent, where three Negresses looked up in stolid indifference to the tragedy being enacted before them.

As Baynes saw his way blocked by the huge Negro, his disappointment and rage filled him with a fury that transformed him into a savage beast. With an oath he leapt on the man before him, hurling him to the ground.

Baynes' fingers shut off a cry for help, but the Negro succeeded in drawing his knife, and an instant later Baynes felt the sharp steel in his shoulder. Again and again the weapon fell.

The white man removed one hand from its choking grip on the black throat. He felt around on the ground beside him, searching for some missile, and at last his fingers touched a stone and closed upon it. Raising it above his antagonist's head the Englishman drove home a terrific blow. Instantly the black relaxed – stunned. Twice more Baynes struck him. Then he leapt to his feet and ran for the goatskin tent.

But before him was another. Naked except for his leopard-skin and his loincloth, Korak slunk into the shadows at the back of Ali ben Kadin's tent. The Arab had just dragged Meriem into the end chamber as Korak's sharp knife slit a six-foot opening in the tent wall. Korak, tall and mighty, sprang through upon the astonished inmates.

Meriem's heart leapt at the sight of the giant figure for which it had hungered for so long.

"Korak!" she cried.

142

"Meriem!"

He uttered the single word as he hurled himself upon the astonished Ali ben Kadin. The three Negresses leapt from their sleeping-mats, screaming. Meriem tried to prevent them from escaping, but the terrified women darted through the hole in the tent and ran screaming through the villlage.

Korak's fingers closed upon the throat of the hideous Ali. His knife plunged into the putrid heart – and Ali ben Kadin lay dead upon the floor of his tent. Korak turned towards Meriem, and at the same moment a bloody and dishevelled apparition burst into the apartment.

"Morison!" cried the girl.

Korak turned and looked at the newcomer. He had been about to take Meriem in his arms, forgetful of all that had happened since he had last seen her. The coming of the young Englishman recalled the scene he had witnessed in the little clearing, and a wave of despair swept over the ape-man.

Already from outside came sounds of the alarm that the three Negresses had started. Men were running towards the tent of Ali ben Kadin. There was no time to be lost.

"Quick!" cried Korak, turning to Baynes. "Take her to the palisade. Here is my rope. With it you can climb the wall and make your escape."

"But you, Korak?" cried Meriem.

"I will remain," replied the ape-man. "I have business with The Sheik."

Meriem hesitated, but Korak seized them both by the shoulders and hustled them through the slit and out into the shadows beyond.

"Now run for it," he ordered, and turned to meet the tribesmen who were pouring into the tent.

The ape-man fought well – fought as he had never fought before, but the odds were too great for victory. Yet he won that which he most craved – time for the

143

Englishman to escape with Meriem. Then he was overwhelmed by numbers and a few minutes later, bound and guarded, was carried to The Sheik's tent.

The old man eyed him in silence for a long time. He was trying to think of some form of torture that would gratify his hatred.

As he sat there looking at Korak the silence was broken by the trumpeting of an elephant in the jungle beyond the palisade. A half smile touched Korak's lips. He turned his head towards the sound and uttered a low, weird call. One of the warriors guarding him struck him across the mouth with the haft of his spear, though none there knew the significance of his cry.

In the jungle Tantor cocked his ears as the sound of Korak's voice fell upon them. He approached the palisade and, lifting his trunk above it, sniffed. Then he placed his head against the wooden logs and pushed, but the palisade was strong and only gave a little to the pressure.

In The Sheik's tent The Sheik rose at last and, pointing at the bound captive, turned to one of his lieutenants.

"Burn him," he commanded, "at once."

The guards dragged Korak to the open space in the centre of the village, where a high stake was set in the ground. To this stake they bound Korak. Then they brought brush and piled it round him, and The Sheik came and stood by to watch the agonies of his victim. But Korak did not wince even after they had fetched a brand and the flames shot up among the dry tinder.

Once again, though, he raised his voice in the low call he had given in The Sheik's tent and now, from beyond the palisade, again came the trumpeting of an elephant.

Old Tantor had been pushing at the palisade in vain. The sound of Korak's voice calling him and the scent of man filled the great beast with rage. He wheeled and shuffled back a dozen paces, then turned and gave voice to a mighty trumpet-call of anger, lowered his head, and charged like a huge battering-ram of flesh and bone and muscle straight for the mighty barrier.

The palisade sagged and splintered under the impact, and through the breach rushed the infuriated bull.

The flames were creeping closer to Korak when one of the blacks heard the noise and turned to see the enormous bulk of Tantor lumbering towards them. The man screamed and fled, and then the bull elephant was among them, tossing Negroes and Arabs to right and left as he tore through the flames to the side of the comrade he loved. The Sheik ran to his tent to get his rifle.

Tantor wrapped his trunk about the body of Korak and the stake to which it was bound, and tore it from the ground. Lifting his burden high above his head, the giant beast wheeled and raced for the breach in the palisade. The Sheik, rifle in hand, rushed from his tent directly into the path of the maddened brute. He raised his weapon but Tantor was upon him, crushing him beneath those gigantic feet as he raced over him.

And then, bearing his burden carefully, Tantor the elephant entered the blackness of the jungle.


Meriem, dazed by the unexpected sight of Korak, permitted herself to be led away by Baynes. He guided her safely to the palisade, and pitched a noose over the top. With difficulty he climbed up, then lowered his hand to assist Meriem.

"Come!" he whispered. "We must hurry."

As though awakened from a sleep, Meriem came to herself. Back there, fighting her enemies alone, was Korak – her Korak. Her place was by his side.

"Go!" she called up to Baynes. "My place is here. You can do no good by remaining. Get away while you can and bring the Big Bwana back with you."

Silently Baynes slid to the ground.

"You are right," he said. "We cannot leave him."

145

"We will go together," said Meriem. "Come!" And she led the way back.

A hundred feet away they saw Korak bound to a stake – the brush piled around him already alight. The Englishman pushed Meriem to one side and started to run for the doomed man. At the same instant Tantor broke through the palisade and charged the group. In the face of the maddened beast the crowd turned and fled, carrying Baynes back with them.

In a moment it was all over, the elephant had disappeared with his prize, and pandemonium reigned throughout the village. Men, women, and children ran helter-skelter for safety. Curs fled, yelping. The horses, camels and donkeys kicked and pulled at their tethers. A dozen or more broke loose, and it was the galloping of these past him that brought a sudden idea into Baynes' head.

"The horses!" he cried. "If we can get a couple of them!"

Instantly Meriem understood and led him to the far end of the village.

"Loosen two of them," she said. "Lead them behind those huts. I will bring saddles and bridles," and before he could stop her she was gone.

Baynes quickly untied two of the restive animals and led them to the hut. Here he saw the girl approaching carrying two saddles. Quickly they placed them on the horses.

Now the girl flung herself into the saddle.

"Hurry!" she whispered. "Ride through the gap that Tantor made."

As she saw Baynes swing his leg over the back of his horse, she shook the reins free. With a lunge, the nervous beast leapt forward.

So sudden was their dash that it carried them halfway across the village before the surprised inhabitants were aware of what was happening. Then an Arab recognized them, and, with a cry of alarm raised his rifle and fired.

The shot was a signal for a volley, and amid the rattle of musketry Meriem and Baynes leapt their flying mounts through the breach in the palisade and galloped up the well-worn trail towards the north.


And Korak?

Tantor carried him deep into the jungle, until no sound from the distant village reached his keen ears. Then he laid his burden gently down. Korak struggled to free himself, but even his great strength was unable to cope with the hard-knotted cord that bound him.

Dawn came, and still Korak was no nearer freedom than before. He began to believe that he would die of thirst and starvation, for he knew that Tantor could not unloose the knots that held him.

And while he struggled through the night with his bonds, Baynes and Meriem were riding rapidly northward along the river. The girl told Baynes that Korak was safe in the jungle with Tantor. It did not occur to her that the ape-man might not be able to burst his bonds. Baynes had been seriously wounded and the girl wanted to get him back to Bwana's home, where he could be properly cared for.

"Then," she said, "I shall get Bwana to come with me and search for Korak. He must come and live with us."

All night they rode, and the day was still young when they came suddenly upon a party hurrying southward. It was Bwana himself and his sleek, black warriors. At sight of Baynes the big Englishman frowned, but he waited to hear Meriem's story before expressing his anger. When she had finished he seemed to have forgotten Baynes. His thoughts were occupied with another subject.

"You say you found Korak?" he asked. "You really saw him?"

"Yes," replied Meriem.

"Did you see him?" He turned to Baynes.

147

"Yes, sir," replied Baynes, "very plainly."

"What does he look like?" continued Bwana.

"I should say he was an Englishman, about my own age," replied Baynes, "though he might be older. He is remarkably muscled, and exceedingly tanned."

"His eyes and hair, did you notice them?" Bwana spoke rapidly. It was Meriem who answered him.

"Korak's hair is black and his eyes are grey," she said. Bwana turned to his headman.

"Take Miss Meriem and Mr. Baynes home," he said. "I am going into the jungle."

"Let me go with you, Bwana," cried Meriem.

"Your place," he said, "is beside the man you love." Then he motioned to his head-man to take his horse and start the return journey to the farm. Meriem slowly mounted the tired Arab that had brought her from the village of The Sheik. A litter was rigged for the now feverish Baynes, and the little cavalcade was soon slowly winding off along the river trail.

Bwana stood watching them until they were out of sight. Not once did Meriem look backward. She rode with bowed head and drooping shoulders. Bwana sighed. He loved the little Arab girl as he might have loved his own daughter. He realized that Baynes had redeemed himself, and so he could not object now if Meriem really loved the man. Yet somehow, some way, Bwana could not convince himself that Baynes was worthy of his little Meriem.

Slowly he turned towards a nearby tree. Leaping up, he caught a branch and drew himself up among the branches. His movements were cat-like and agile. High into the tree he made his way and there, began to take off his clothing. From the game-bag slung across one shoulder he drew a long strip of doeskin, a neatly coiled rope, and a wicked-looking knife. The doeskin he fashioned into a loincloth, the rope he looped over one shoulder, and the knife he thrust into his belt.

When he stood erect, his head thrown back and his great

chest expanded, a grim smile touched his lips for a moment, his grey eyes narrowed. He crouched and leapt to a lower limb, and was away through the trees towards the south-east. He moved swiftly, stopping occasionally to raise his voice in a weird and piercing scream and listen for a reply.

He had travelled for several hours when, ahead of him, he heard a faint response – the cry of a bull ape answering his cry. His nerves tingled as the sound fell upon his ears. Again he voiced his hideous call and sped forward.

Korak, finally convinced that he must die if he remained where he was, spoke to Tantor in the strange tongue that the great beast understood. He commanded the elephant to lift him and carry him towards the north-east. There, recently, Korak had seen both white men and black. If he could come upon one of the latter it would be a simple matter to command Tantor to capture the fellow, and then Korak could get him to release him from the stake.

As Tantor bore him along through the forest Korak called aloud now and then in the hope of attracting Akut's band of anthropoids, whose wanderings often brought them into this neighbourhood. Akut, he thought, would be able to untie the knots – and Akut, to the south of him, heard his calls faintly, and came. There was another who heard them too.

After Bwana had left his party, sending them back towards the farm, Meriem rode for a short distance with bowed head.

Suddenly she called the head-man to her.

"I am going back with Bwana," she announced.

The black shook his head. "No!" he replied. "Bwana says I take you home. So I take you home."

"You refuse to let me go?" asked the girl.

The native nodded, and fell to the rear where he could

149

watch her. Meriem half smiled. Presently her horse passed beneath a low-hanging branch, and suddenly the head-man found himself gazing at the girl's empty saddle.

Meriem raced straight back towards a place where she knew the elephants often gathered – deep in the forest. She moved silently and swiftly. Her only thought was that she must reach Korak and bring him back with her.

She had been travelling rapidly for several hours without rest when she heard ahead of her the familiar cry of a great ape calling to his kind. She did not reply, but only increased her speed until she almost flew. Now she picked up Tantor's spoor and knew she was on the right trail. All at once Meriem caught sight of them as the great elephant shuffled ahead balancing the man and the heavy stake upon his head, holding them there with his up-curled trunk.

"Korak!" cried Meriem.

Instantly the bull swung round, lowered his burden to the ground and, trumpeting savagely, prepared to defend his comrade. The ape-man, recognizing the girl's voice, felt a sudden lump in his throat.

"Meriem!" he called back.

Happily the girl clambered to the ground and ran forward to release Korak, but Tantor lowered his head ominously and trumpeted a warning.

"Go back! Go back!" cried Korak. "He will kill you."

Meriem paused. "Tantor!" she called to the huge brute. "Don't you remember me? I am Meriem. I used to ride on your broad back."

The bull only rumbled in his throat and shook his tusks in angry defiance. Then Korak tried to order him away, so that the girl could approach and release him, but Tantor would not go. He saw in every human except Korak an enemy. He thought the girl wanted to harm his friend, and he would take no chances.

Then Korak hit upon a scheme. "Pretend to go away," he called to the girl. "Keep downwind from us so that

Tantor won't get your scent, then follow us. After a while I'll have him put me down, and find some pretext for sending him away. While he is gone you can slip up and cut my bonds – have you a knife?"

"Yes, I have a knife," she replied. "I'll go now – I think we may be able to fool him, but don't be too sure – Tantor invented cunning."

In a moment she had disappeared. The elephant listened, and raised his trunk to catch her scent. Korak commanded him to raise him once more and proceed upon their way. After a moment's hesitation Tantor did as he was bid. It was then that Korak heard the distant call of an ape.

"Akut!" he thought. "Good! Tantor knows Akut well. He will let him approach."

Raising his voice Korak replied to the call of the ape, but he let Tantor move off with him through the jungle – it would do no harm to try the other plan.

They came to a clearing and Korak smelt water. He ordered Tantor to lay him down, and fetch water in his trunk. The big beast placed him on the grass in the centre of the clearing, then stood with cocked ears searching for danger. There seemed none, and he moved towards the little brook some two or three hundred yards away.

The animal ambled off across the clearing and disappeared in the jungle beyond. There, though, he wheeled round and came cautiously back to the edge of the clearing where he could see without being seen. Tantor, by nature was suspicious. He still feared the return of the she Tarmangani who had attempted to attack his Korak. He would stand there and assure himself that all was well before he continued towards the water.

Ah! It was well that he did! There she was now dropping from the branches of a tree and running swiftly towards the ape-man.

Tantor waited. He would let her reach Korak before he charged – that would ensure she had no chance of escape. His little eyes blazed savagely. Meriem was almost

151

at Korak's side when Tantor saw the long knife in her hand, and then he broke forth from the jungle, bellowing horribly, and charged down upon the frail girl.

## Tarzan's Return

Korak screamed commands to his huge protector in an effort to halt him, but all to no avail. Meriem raced towards the trees with all the speed that lay in her swift feet, but Tantor drove down upon her with the rapidity of an express train.

He was almost upon her now. Korak wanted to close his eyes, but he could not. His throat was dry and parched. Never in all his savage existence had he suffered such horror – never before had he known what terror meant. A dozen more strides and the brute would seize her.

Korak's eyes almost started from their sockets. A strange figure had leapt from the tree beyond the girl, straight into the path of the charging elephant! It was a naked white giant.

With empty hands he faced the maddened Tantor. A sharp command broke from the stranger's lips – the great beast halted in his tracks – and Meriem swung upward into the tree to safety. Korak fastened his eyes upon the face of Meriem's deliverer, and as recognition came they went wide in incredulity and surprise.

Meriem was watching too, and wondering. Suddenly the man turned. "Come, Meriem!" he called, and then she recognized him with a startled "Bwana!"

Quickly the girl dropped from the tree and ran to his side. Together the two walked to where Korak lay, his eyes wide with wonder and in them a pathetic appeal for forgiveness.

"Jack!" cried the white giant, kneeling at the ape-man's side.

"Father!" came chokingly from Korak's lips.

Quickly the man cut the bonds that held Korak, and as the youth leapt to his feet, the older man turned to Meriem.

"I thought," he said, "I told you to return to the farm?"

Meriem looked pleadingly into Bwana's eyes.

"You told me," she said, in a very small voice, "that my place was beside the man I loved." She turned towards Korak, her eyes filled with the wonderful light that no other man had ever seen in them.

Korak fell upon one knee before her and lifting her hand to his lips kissed it.

A rumble from Tantor brought them to instant alertness. Tantor was looking at the trees behind them, and as their eyes followed his gaze the head and shoulders of a great ape appeared amidst the foliage.

For a moment the creature eyed them, then from its throat rose a loud scream of joy. The beast leapt to the ground, followed by a score of bulls, and waddled towards them shouting: "Tarzan has returned! Tarzan, Lord of the Jungle!"

It was Akut, and instantly he began to leap and bound about the trio.

Korak laid his hand affectionately upon his father's shoulder.

"There is only one Tarzan," he said. "There can never be another."

Two days later the three dropped from the trees on the edge of the plain, from where they could see the bungalow.

Tarzan of the Apes had regained his civilized clothing from the tree where he had hidden it. Korak, however, refused to meet his mother in the savage raiment that he had worn so long and as Meriem would not leave him,

153

Tarzan went ahead to the bungalow for horses and clothes.

My Dear met him at the gate, her eyes filled with sorrow, for she saw that Meriem was not with him.

"Where is she?" she asked, her voice trembling. "Muviri told me she disobeyed your instructions and ran off into the jungle. Oh, John, I cannot bear to lose her too!" And Lady Greystoke broke down and wept.

Lord Greystoke looked down into her eyes, his own smiling and filled with the light of happiness.

"What is it, John?" she cried. "You have good news – do not keep me waiting for it."

"The best news that ever came to either of us," he said.

She cried, "You have found – her?" She could not bring herself to hope for the impossible.

"Yes, Jane," he said, and his voice was husky with emotion. "I have found her, and – *him!*"

"Where is he? Where are they?" she demanded.

"Out there at the edge of the jungle. He wouldn't come to you in his leopard-skin and nakedness – he sent me to fetch civilized clothing."

She clapped her hands in ecstasy, and turned towards the bungalow. "Wait!" she cried over her shoulder. "I have all his suits – I have saved them all. I will bring one to you."

Tarzan laughed and called to her to stop.

"The only clothing on the place that will fit him," he said, "is mine – your little boy has grown, Jane."

And so, an hour later, Korak rode home to his mother and found in her arms and eyes the love and forgiveness that he craved for.

And then the mother turned to Meriem, an expression of pitying sorrow on her face.

"My little girl," she said, "in the midst of our happiness a great sorrow awaits you – Morison did not survive his wounds."

The sorrow in Meriem's eyes expressed only what she

sincerely felt, but it was not the sorrow of a woman bereft of her beloved.

"I am sorry," she said quite simply. "But I did not love him, you know. I did not even know what love was until I knew that Korak lived," and she turned towards The Killer with a smile.

Lady Greystoke looked quickly into the eyes of her son – the son who one day would be Lord Greystoke. She wanted to know that Jack loved the little Arab waif too. The look in his eyes answered the question in her heart, and she threw her arms about them both and kissed them each a dozen times.

"Now," she cried, "I really have a daughter!"


It was several weary marches to the nearest mission, but they only waited a few days to rest before setting out upon the journey. After the marriage ceremony had been performed they kept on to the coast to take passage for England.

Those days were the most wonderful of Meriem's life. She had not dreamed even vaguely of the marvels that civilization held in store for her. The great ocean and the steamship filled her with awe.

They had been home only a week when Lord Greystoke received a message from his old friend, D'Arnot.

It was in the form of a letter of introduction brought by one General Armand Jacot. Lord Greystoke recalled the name, for Jacot was in reality the Prince de Cadrenet – that intense republican who refused to use a title that had belonged to his family for four hundred years.

Lord Greystoke received the hawk-nosed, grey-moustached soldier in his library.

"I have come to you," explained General Jacot, "because I am told there is no one more intimately acquainted with Central Africa than you.

"Let me tell you my story from the beginning. Many years ago my little daughter was stolen, presumably by

155

Arabs, while I was serving with the Foreign Legion in Algeria. We did all that love and money could do to discover her, but to no avail. Never did we find a man or woman who had seen her since the day she mysteriously disappeared.

"A week ago, however, there came to me in Paris an Arab, who called himself Abdul Kamak. He said he had found my daughter and could lead me to her."

"What proof did the Arab bring that she was your daughter?" asked Lord Greystoke.

"None," replied the other. "That is why D'Arnot and I thought it best to consult you before organizing an expedition. The fellow had only an old photograph of her, on the back of which was pasted a newspaper cutting describing her and offering a reward."

"Have you the photograph with you?" asked Lord Greystoke.

The General drew an envelope from his pocket, took a yellowed photograph from it, and handed it to the Englishman.

Lord Greystoke examined the photograph for a moment, then a queer expression entered his eyes. He touched a bell at his elbow, and an instant later a footman entered.

"Ask my son's wife if she will be so good as to come to the library," he directed. A moment later Meriem entered.

General Jacot took one look at her then turned to Lord Greystoke.

"It is Jeanne," said Jacot, shaking with suppressed emotion, "but she does not recognize me – of course she could not." Then he turned to Meriem. "My child," he said, "I am your –"

But she interrupted him with a quick, glad cry as she ran towards him with outstretched arms.

"I know you! I know you!" she cried. "Oh, now I remember," and the old man folded her in his arms.

Jack Clayton and his mother were summoned, and

when the story had been told they were overjoyed that Meriem had found a father and a mother.

"And really you didn't marry an Arab waif after all," said Meriem. "Isn't it fine!"

"You are fine," replied Korak. "I married my little Meriem, and I don't care whether she is an Arab or just a little Tarmangani."

"She is neither, my son," said General Armand Jacot. "She is a princess in her own right."

# TARZAN THE MIGHTY

Tarzan was "born" in the mind of his author, the late Edgar Rice Burroughs, over fifty years ago. Since then hundreds of millions of Tarzan books have been published in many languages, and Tarzan has been featured in dozens of films. Now, of course, there is a Tarzan television series.

Dragon books have secured the publication rights to a whole series of these thrilling Tarzan adventure stories, and will issue them in the course of the next few months. They have all been "adapted" to make for easier reading. "Adapting" means that they have been abridged, because it was felt that they might then be more acceptable to young modern readers.

But the stories are still Edgar Rice Burroughs' – his was the genius that gave us this wonderful character, this jungle man who could live with the beasts of the forest and defend himself even against the mightiest of enemies.

Four Tarzan stories have now been published in the Dragon series – *Tarzan of the Apes, The Return of Tarzan, The Beasts of Tarzan* and *The Son of Tarzan*. At least twelve more Tarzan titles will appear as Dragon books in the next few months.

They are wonderful stories, thrilling and fascinating. You should start with Number 1, *Tarzan of the Apes*, and work your way right through the series! Don't give your Tarzans away either, for you will want to read them over and over again!

Now, look out for the other exciting Tarzans *and ask for them from your bookseller or newsagent.*

If you have difficulty in obtaining these or any other Dragon books, you may obtain them from Dragon Books, 11 New Fetter Lane, London, E.C.4. They will be sent to you post-free on receipt of 2s. 10d. per book.